The Girl

I Am,

Was,

and Never
Will Be

For Erin Powers
and for Boisey Collins Jr.,
both on the other side of something
just beyond view.

"... narratives ... pull us through to the next realm, or the parallel universe, or the future in which we are the protagonists."

—adrienne maree brown

"I had been an empty space, and now I was finding a language, a story to shape myself by. I had been alone and now there were others."

—Linda Hogan

"Since 1975 I too had many hopes, wishes, wonderings, imaginings, etc. etc., re: Shannon (who I still know as Erin)."

—Patricia Powers

The Girl

I Am,

Was,

and Never
Will Be

DUTTON BOOKS

An imprint of Penguin Random House LLC, New York

First published in the United States of America by Dutton Books,
an imprint of Penguin Random House LLC, 2023

Visit us online at penguinrandomhouse.com.

Library of Congress Cataloging-in-Publication Data is available.

Printed in the United States of America

ISBN 9780593111994

1st Printing

LSCH
Design by Anna Booth
Text set in Sabon LT Std

The Girl

I Am,

Was,

and Never

Will Be

A Speculative Memoir of Transracial Adoption

Shannon Gibney

DUTTON BOOKS

Prologue

I WAS BORN January 30, 1975, in Ann Arbor, Michigan.

The name on my birth certificate is Shannon Gibney, and my parents are listed as Jim and Susan Gibney. These are my white adoptive parents, who raised me. They gave me the loafers I remember wearing almost forty years ago. The backyard woods where my imagination first grew roots was theirs.

The woman who gave birth to me and subsequently relinquished me was named Patricia Powers. She was a white, working-class Irish American woman who had a short relationship with my African American birth father, Boisey Collins Jr. My birth mother named me Erin Powers after I was born, but I didn't find that out until I was nineteen. I possess no childhood memories of either of them.

I grew up with my white adopted parents in Ann Arbor, Michigan, with two white brothers, who were biologically related to my parents. When I was nineteen and no longer a child in the eyes of the state, I embarked on a search for my possible birth siblings and my birth parents. I found my birth mother, Patricia Powers, who then still lived in her hometown of Utica, New York. We had a complicated, on-again, off-again relationship from the mid-nineties until her death from cancer in 2014. She was fifty-eight when she passed.

Through my search, I also discovered that my birth father, Boisey Collins Jr., died from complications due to injuries he sustained during a high-speed police chase in Palo Alto, California, in 1981, when I was six. He was thirty-five at the time of his death.

I discovered many other things through my search and reunion experiences. I did not discover many things, as well. (I keep that particular hunger at bay with scraps of speculation.)

I now have two living children of my own, Boisey and Marwein, and one dead, Sianneh.

This is one way to tell the story, in this time, in this place.

What follows are other ways to tell the stories of Shannon and Erin, the known and the unknown, truth and speculation, to awaken the sleepers, to call forth the living, the dead, and those residing elsewhere.

NOVEMBER 1994.

Letter from Patricia Powers to Shannon Gibney.

Shannon, I must inform you of the following - he
you must be diligent in your own self-breast exam
(do it monthly), and for you to obtain a baseline
mammogram (even though you're in your 20's) - don't
let your primary healthcare provider tell you
otherwise. As you may or may not recall your
biological grandmother had breast cancer for which she
underwent left mastectomy 2 yrs ago (yes, she is now
considered "a survivor"- however the 5-year mark is
still considered monumental). Since your biological
grandmother was orphaned @ 12 yrs of age, we have <u>no</u>
<u>family history pre-your grandmother</u> (this is important
is assessing & risk. However, I, over the years, have
undergone <u>3</u> surgical breast biopsies - the pathology
reports from these biopsies <u>and</u> the fact that my
mother had breast cancer places me @ a higher risk for
breast cancer. (I recently have been accepted as a candidate
for the International <u>STAR Program</u> study - a longitudinal,
double-blind study which follows higher-risk for breast CA
♀'s over years, while placing us on either Tamoxifen or
Raloxifen (these are breast cancer prevention meds), and
performs closely-monitored exams (quite involved - we can
discuss further). I have not yet agreed to participate
in this study d/t major side-effects of above-mentioned
drugs. <u>The consequence of this information for you is:</u>

① You <u>must</u> do monthly-self-breast exams to get to know
    your breasts so-to-speak, and assess any abnormalities
    early. (If you do not know how to do this or feel
    uncomfortable about it, I can send you a teaching pamphlet
    and/or verbally discuss it with you.

② Obtain a <u>Baseline Mammography</u>! Your primary care MD or
    Nurse Practitioner must order this. Do not let them tell you

Shannon, I must inform you of the following [illegible]: you must be diligent in your own self-breast exam (do it monthly), and for you to obtain a baseline mammogram (even though you're in your 20's)—don't let your primary healthcare provider tell you otherwise. As you may or may not recall your biological grandmother had breast cancer for which she underwent left mastectomy 2 years ago (yes, she is now considered "a survivor"—however the 5-year mark is still considered monumental). Since your biological grandmother was orphaned @ 12 yrs of age, we have <u>no family history pre-your grandmother</u> (this is important in assessing women's risk. However, I, over the years, have undergone <u>3</u> surgical breast biopsies—the pathology reports from these biopsies <u>and</u> the fact that my mother had breast cancer places me @ a higher risk for breast cancer. [. . .]

The consequence of this information for you is:

1. *You <u>must</u> do monthly self-breast exams to get to know your breasts so-to-speak, and assess any abnormalities early. (If you do not know how to do this or feel uncomfortable about it, I can send you a teaching pamphlet and/or verbally discuss it with you.)*

2. *Obtain a <u>Baseline Mammography:</u> Your primary care MD or Nurse Practitioner must order this. Do not let them tell you are too young (many MD's remain uninformed <u>and</u> misinformed about this). My first breast lump was discovered when I was 22 years old. Mammographies are slightly uncomfortable, but expose you to less radiation than an x-ray. Just make sure wherever you go, they use what is called <u>low-dose mammography.</u>*

Family History to tell your health provider:

a) *Biological Grandmother with breast cancer (older family history unknown due to grandmother being orphaned).*
b) *Biological mother @ higher-risk for breast cancer: More info on me can be sent if needed.*
c) *2 biological Aunts (Kathleen and Bridget) @ higher risk.*
d) *Your biological 2nd cousin with breast cancer (now expired).*

Shannon, this health history is not intended to frighten you in any way. It is intended to inform you so you may have as much control over this unfortunate health issue as possible. Feel free to discuss all of this with your Mom . . . She may call me or write if she would like—to better inform both of you. You may not be @ higher-risk at all, but it's important for you to follow-through with mammography and to do self-breast exam.

Unfortunately, I have no knowledge of your biological father's family history. I would however advise you to contact them to try to find out if there is a family history of breast cancer, particularly in your biological grandmother. (Remember though that men get breast cancer too).

Erin Powers is nineteen.

ERIN SITS DOWN ON THE FRONT STOOP, wraps her arms around her sharp knees, and then lays her head across them sideways. From this vantage point she can see her neighbors Phil and Alice having a fight on their porch across the street. She blinks and then feels her mascara dripping down the side of her face from the heat. She wipes it away with the back of her hand. She doesn't know where she will sleep tonight, but she knows it will not be in her own bed.

Her mother has just thrown her out, she says for her own good. She discovered Erin's transcript from her second semester at Utica College, hidden at the bottom of her underwear drawer, clearly listing Fs beside each class, because she did not attend and did not do the work. *You are probably the most brilliant person I have ever met, and you just waste all of it . . . Why? I will never understand you. I sacrificed everything for you, and yet you choose to spit in my face . . .*

Her mother who is dying of a cancer of unknown origin. Her mother who will not submit to further tests that everyone says are necessary, much less treatment. Patricia Powers: a rebel to the very end. Or maybe a rebel heralding her own ending?

When Mom speaks like this to her, Erin has to concentrate on balling her hands into tight fists, and commanding them to stay at her sides, because what she really wants to do is sock her in the mouth— hard. *I finally got my life in order, after so many years of messing it up so royally, and I wish you could support me by not wasting yours. After all, you are the one who knows the costs of living with a drunk most intimately.* And now, she will get to understand the costs of dying with a drunk most intimately.

Erin thinks of the girl then, Other-Erin-Who-Is-Not-Erin, and wonders if she has lived with a white mother who should have been better, who so many times could have *chosen* to be better, but did not . . . Is she also looking for her Absent Black Father (and by extension, her Blackness) or at least for a sibling who could relate, and instead coming up against wall after wall, her dying mother and white family understanding none of it?

At least I have Essie is what always comes to her in these moments. Essie always with the *Eat some more, Flaquísima,* at her family dinner table, eyeing Erin's tiny wrists and ever-angular face with worry. Essie of the *We'll find something this time, I can feel it,* every time Erin drags her to some random county office in the middle of a cornfield, tracking down a lead on some tiny bit of information about her father. Essie of *You're Black, Flaca, just accept it. Like I'm Mexican. Plain to see if you just use your eyes. Fuck 'em, Erin, even if they're your family. White people are wack. But that's not your fault.*

Erin stands up, dusting off her bright red silk jumper dress. She found it at a vintage shop and wears it frequently over T-shirts. She would like a cigarette right about now, but she'll die before she goes back into that house and wakes her mother. No. Essie. Essie will let her bunk on the floor of the apartment she shares with three other girls near Mohawk Community College. It might not be comfortable, but it will work for the time being. And in her nineteen years, Erin has become a master of making broken things work. She starts walking, kicking up stones and stepping on cracks in the sidewalk with each step.

PART ONE

Recursive selves, infinite pathways

WHAT IS A STORY, if not a set of particular details, in a particular space and time, with particular people—all of it porous, weaving in and out of other stories (both broken and whole) in time, place, and space?

What is a family, if not a set of relations that people in powerful institutions create, transform, or dissolve through official documents?

What is a brother, if not you who I say is my brother?

What is a birth mother, but a secondary character in a story that never concludes?

The only way for people like me—adoptees—to express the truth of our lives and experiences is to embrace that there are no singular truths. There is no one reality. There are no stories without holes. There are only spaces to be breathed into. Sometimes, rewritten. Always, the spaces are revered. And feared.

There are connections. Powerful ones that seem to generate their own energy capable of spanning divides of space and time. And there is always something on the other side of the divide. In my imagination, the energy is a spiral emitting hot sparks and with a core of possibility that I can't help but be drawn to, just as I'm drawn to my own face in a mirror. Some aspect of adoptees' birth stories that gnaws at us because it just doesn't make sense. Some tale of our origins too blurry to be seen or understood. In many ways, this is why the speculative realm of wormholes and timelines intersecting exists for many of us near or beside our "real lives." Who would I be now if I had been raised in Korea? How many birth siblings do I have out there? Do they look like me? Laugh like me? What would it really have been like if my birth parents raised me? Would I know to ask a doctor for a mammogram before it's too late? In this way, the speculative is not conjecture for adoptees. The speculative is our "real lives."

I may have imbibed a steady stream of *Flash Gordon, Star Wars*, and *Star Trek* growing up, and like so many children, incorporated those fantastical elements of travel through space and time, portals to multiple dimensions and universes, time loops, and whatnot into my sense of the world. I may have played imaginary games with my brothers and cousins and friends out in the woods behind our house in Ann Arbor, and worried that I spotted a rip in the fabric of space-time on the ground. I may have wondered if there were other *me*'s in these adjacent universes, and thought about what I would say to them if I ever met them, how I would see them, if they could see me. Always, I wondered if they felt as strange as I did, a mixed Black girl in a white family with just a little bit of knowledge of what was on the other side of the divide in my story: my birth mother's story, my birth father's story, the *me*'s they knew only briefly. How did all these stories, this mad mix of knowns and unknowns, touch us?

Memory

A reader of an early draft asks, "Are the loafers you and Erin share a very specific memory for you? Is there any chance there's a picture of you wearing them?"

I shuffle toward my now-busted childhood scrapbook, elementary school certificates of achievement and withered school-year photos falling out its edges. I flip through the coarse construction-paper pages. And it is then that I see it. "OMG, I've totally seen that look from the first picture on my daughter's face . . ."

Shannon (second from left, in loafers) rehearsing a fourth-grade production of *Mary Poppins*.

Point of View

I AM ERIN, I say in my head.

I am Erin, she says in my head.

I am Erin, Shannon says in her head.

I am Erin, Shannon says in my head.

Shannon is Erin, I say in her head.

I am she, Erin says in Shannon's head.

The girl I could have been, says Shannon. *The girl I am,* says Erin. *The girl I never was, but could always see.*

The two timelines, the two me's *existing at the point of a wormhole,* they both say.

Erin? Shannon asks.

Shannon? Erin asks.

I am Shannon, I say in my head.

I am Shannon, she says in my head.

I am Shannon, Erin says in her head.

I am Shannon, Erin says in my head.

Erin is Shannon, I say in her head.

I am she, Shannon says in Erin's head.

The girl I could have been . . .

Erin Powers is ten.

HER MOTHER IS STILL ASLEEP, but her mother is always asleep these days. The girl has a bright red jumper on over navy corduroy pants that her grandmother pressed for her the night before. The girl's loafers are worn and stained, but she likes them that way because she can play kickball in them so much better at recess. When they were new last year, her feet slipped, and when she kicked the ball, her shoe would always go flying. Now, though, the hand-me-down, synthetic leather shoes pinch her toes. They are like second skin, sticking to her feet exactly, stopping and going when she needs them to.

The morning is hazy and bright, the early fall clouds spanning the horizon. As she skips down the battered concrete steps of their apartment building, the girl resists the urge to scream at the top of her lungs. She doesn't know exactly why she wants to do this. It's just a feeling that will engulf her at random moments in her day, moments that she can't predict. This sense of the bigness of the world, how much of it there is beyond her reach—and its essential goodness as well. But the girl knows that shouting like this, in the quiet lower-middle-class neighborhood that her aunts and uncles and grandmother have worked so hard to get her and her mother into, would be frowned upon, and she is already weary of the many frowns and questioning glances she and her mother get when they walk together anywhere here.

A silver Trans Am rumbles by on the street, its exhaust too loud for so early in the morning. The girl notices the unfamiliar blue license plate and the bumper sticker that reads "Go Blue."

Six minutes before the bus comes. Six minutes to dawdle to the end of the block, dodging cracks in the sidewalk so as not to *break your mother's back*. Six minutes to taunt the Evans' dim-witted wolfhound. Her mother has told her on many occasions to *leave that dog alone, you never know what a dog can do, even if it is securely tethered to a chain*. But the girl never listens to her mother. Except when she hits her.

"Erin!" a voice calls out brightly behind her.

The girl—who is me, who was me, who was not me, who could have been me—turns around to face the voice. "Essie!" she answers, equally brightly. Essie is short for Esmeralda, a name that Erin finds far more beautiful, but that Essie insists she will never respond to. "It's a vieja name," she will say, twisting her nose into a knot and frowning. Like many children, Erin understands the feeling behind the words in languages she doesn't speak—enjoys their gliding and sometimes raucous flow, even when she does not know their literal meaning. When she is around Essie and her family, running through the neighborhood before her mother gets home from work, eating chicharrones and quesadillas and rice and beans with the family, she feels like she fits right in with the *que*s and the *si*s and the *flaco*s and the *buen dia, mi amor*s. Although she can't reply or participate in the conversation, she strangely feels more at ease with the Martinezes than she does with her own family. She doesn't know why this is, only that it is true. And that it has something to do with the brownness of her skin and the bubble of scream in her throat that the ever-expansive world elicits now and then, and that it also has something to do with the look in her mother's eyes when she finds out she has been *over there again*.

"My mom said I had to wear a sweater this morning," Essie says, running up to the girl breathlessly. She shrugs, and pulls at the sleeves of an ugly yellow sweater. Erin wonders if Essie found it in the same pile of worn sweaters she and her mother were looking through at Goodwill last weekend. "Ugh," Essie says. "I'm hot already."

The girl nods. "Sorry."

Essie looks sideways at her friend, her bright red short-sleeve jumper lighting up the block. "You're lucky your mom never makes you wear stuff," she says.

"Yeah." The truth is that the girl has been dressing herself since she could walk, because her mother never showed any interest in what she was or was not wearing, and is unconscious most of the time she is home anyway.

Essie glances back at her house furtively. "Once the bus comes, I'm taking this junk off. They can't see what they can't see."

Erin laughs. "You got something on under it, right?"

Essie pushes her playfully. Gillian and Jack are already at the bus stop, a few feet in front of them. They are twins and are mostly obnoxious, so Essie and Erin want nothing to do with them. "No, I'm just gonna take it off and show it all to everyone," says Essie.

Erin laughs, and thrusts her chest out. "¡Hola, chicos! ¡Soy La Bella! ¡Besame mucho!" She puckers up and makes loud kissing noises.

Essie collapses in giggles. "Ay, if Matilda saw you!" Matilda is Essie's older sister. She is sixteen and *a pain in the ass*, as Essie's brother says out of earshot of their parents. Always prancing around in too-short skirts and too-tight shirts, with way too much makeup—things that her parents will never let her wear out of the house. That is why there is always so much shouting.

Gillian, who always wears her hair in two perfect braids, looks disgusted. "You're weird," she tells the girls as they approach.

Essie rolls her eyes.

But Erin can never help opening her mouth in moments like these. ("It's why you're your mother's daughter," her aunt Bridget is fond of telling her.)

"At least we're not ugly," Erin tells Gillian, whose face immediately colors at the insult.

Gillian is, in fact, not ugly at all. Gillian has perfectly white skin, and perfectly blue eyes, and perfectly symmetrical features. She has many friends, especially among the white girls, and all the boys have crushes on her. Which is why Erin revels in the perverse joy of making her question all of her basic assumptions of her self-worth.

"I'm—I'm not ugly!" Gillian exclaims incredulously as the bus pulls up.

The brakes exhale loudly, and the front doors open, beckoning them up the steps.

Erin leaps on, saluting the bus driver, who looks half-asleep as usual. "I never said you were," she throws back at Gillian over her shoulder.

Essie shakes her head. "You so bad," she whispers in her friend's ear. It is something she will repeat, a phrase that will bind them together through time and space and circumstance, throughout their lives, in moments like these when Erin can't seem to help being anyone other than Erin, and Essie is sole witness to how much this irrepressible Erin-ness dominates others.

Erin just grins, then finds them a seat in the back.

"No, you have to carry the number across the top, then add it to what's already there. Like this," says Jared, scribbling across the paper furiously. There are four of them in the fourth-grade advanced math group, two girls and two boys, none of them friends. Every day they must complete some kind of boring worksheet together, and then spend the rest of the class helping the students in the lower groups finish theirs. Erin finds it all unbearably tiresome, which is why she has her *Robotech* comic under the desk. She *thinks* she is being surreptitious, but she grunts every single time a robot vaporizes a Zentraedi, and she hasn't looked at the calculations on the math sheet once.

Kelly sighs and sits back in her chair, arms crossed.

Liam looks from Kelly to Jared to Erin and shakes his head. The girl notices but keeps her eyes on the comic. The humans are just now beginning to realize the power of protoculture energy. It's getting good.

Out of the corner of her eye, she sees Essie make a face at her across the room. Essie is stuck in the dumb kids' math group, just because she speaks Spanish and is Mexican. Erin knows she is bored out of her mind because so is she.

At Erin's last conference, Mrs. Harris had sat with her and her mother, hands clasped together so tightly in front of her you could see the white of her knuckles, lips pursed together in a thin red line. "I just don't understand it," Mrs. Harris said. "How a child so obviously intelligent could be so dead set against learning. I'm doing everything in my power to make sure she is academically challenged, but all I get is attitude."

At this, Erin felt a slight smile creep out the side of her mouth, but one glance at her tired and fed-up mother smothered it immediately. "Oh, so you think this is funny?" her mother had said, taking her chin in her hand sharply.

The girl had shaken her head vigorously. "No."

Kelly and Jared finally get it together enough to finish the work-sheet, with Liam's help. The two boys protest when Erin feigns interest at the end and wants to write her name beside theirs for credit. But Kelly slides the sheet over to her in a gesture of feminine solidarity, and Erin signs with a flourish and a smile. She has successfully avoided reproach. Again.

"How was school today?" Mom asks her later, taking a long drag of her cigarette. She has just gotten home from her shift and is still wearing her scrubs. Her dirty blond hair is pulled back into a messy pony-tail, and dark circles hang under her eyes.

"Fine," says Erin absently. She is seated in front of the television in the sofa chair, munching on pretzels. *Robotech* was on a half hour ago, and now she is on to *The Smurfs*, which is a sorry substitute but will have to do.

"You listening better to Mrs. Harris, right?" Mom asks.

Erin knows that Mom will turn off the television in another minute if she doesn't pretend to pay attention, so she forces herself to look at her, and plasters a pleasant expression on her face. "Yep," she says evenly. "Got a perfect score on my spelling test." This isn't a complete lie. She got seventy-five percent on this week's spelling test, but she did ace one two weeks ago.

"Oh, really?" her mother says. Her tone is not quite incredulous but not quite congratulatory, either. "What were some of the words on it?" Then she's seized by a coughing fit. She is having more of those lately. After witnessing one at the park a few weeks ago, Essie told Erin, *You really got to get your mother to quit.* Erin had just laughed and said that it would be more likely for Reagan to run as a Democrat. Essie had narrowed her eyes and then rode off on her Huffy Sweet Thunder, which did make Erin regret her response a bit. But Erin knew what Erin knew, and that was that her mother would never quit smoking. Or drinking, for that matter. It was just part of her, like her low growl of a laugh or her obsession with the news. Some things you just couldn't change about people.

Her mother finally gets control of the cough, leans over the sink, and spits mucus.

"Disgusting," Erin says under her breath. But she pretends not to see. Even though her mother has to know she witnesses this display in their tiny apartment, it still feels wrong to acknowledge it somehow. Her mother's weakness. She works so hard to pretend it is not there. This is something they have in common.

Mom takes a glass from the cupboard and fills it from the tap. She sips it tentatively, then comes back into the living room.

On the screen, Papa Smurf is busy chastising Grouchy Smurf for eating all his sarsaparilla. But Grouchy Smurf is not having it. Erin loves Grouchy, because he doesn't take it from anyone—even Papa.

"So?" Mom asks her again.

Erin can't stop the frown spreading across her face. Why can't she just let her watch her show already and call Aunt Bridget or Aunt Kathleen if she really wants to talk to someone? She giggles as Lazy Smurf polishes off the last of the sarsaparilla while Papa and Grouchy are distracted by their arguing.

Mom sighs. She takes the rubber band out of her hair and lets it fall around her face. Then she combs it out with her fingers—something she does when she's agitated. "Erin," she says. "I'm talking to you."

Erin laughs again. Papa and Grouchy have just gotten wise to Lazy and have started chasing him.

Mom reaches over and turns off the television.

"Hey! I was watching that."

Mom leans over, so her face is just inches from Erin's, so that the burnt smell of cigarettes seems to ooze from every pore. "And I'm talking to you, young lady."

Erin crosses her arms and leans back in her chair. "*Expression* and *repetition*." Then she stares right at Mom, unflinching.

"What?" Mom backs up a bit.

Erin sighs dramatically. "The words on the spelling test. You know, your super-important question?" She can't help the attitude that seeps into her voice, even though she knows it will probably get her in more trouble.

"Watch it, young lady," says Mom.

"What?" Erin asks, feigning ignorance.

Just then the phone rings.

"Can I turn my show back on now? Please?" Erin asks.

Mom shoots her a look. "Absolutely not," she says. "Just go . . .
read or something."

Erin sighs again dramatically. "But I've finished all the books we
got at the library last week!" She has actually finished all the books
she *liked* from the library trip last week. Everyone told her she would
absolutely loooove Bridge to Terabithia, but she found it boring and
had put it down forty pages in.

Mom picks up the phone, and her voice changes immediately. "Oh,
heeeeyyyy! Yes, I'm good. How are *you*?" She's actually smiling now,
and as she carries the phone and its cradle into the other room, her
whole being seems to shift dramatically.

I roll my eyes. It's got to be Katie or Carrie or whoever the new
woman Mom is seeing is.

"No, yeah, that'd be fun," I hear her say in the other room.

Which means she probably has a date this weekend. Which isn't all
bad, I realize, perking up. Because that means I can go over to Essie's
and maybe even sleep over. I won't have to battle Mom about it, since
Mom doesn't want Aunt Bridget or Aunt Kathleen or Uncle Jim or
Grandma or anyone in the family to know about her dates. Which she
would have to explain or lie about if she asked them to watch Erin. "It's
just better this way," she'll say to me sometimes, after a long drag on
her cigarette. "Trust me."

In the bathroom mirror, after brushing her teeth, Erin looks at her face.
It is light brown—similar to Essie's but yellower in tone. Her eyes are
friendly and open, although mischief also lurks in their depths. She
has her mother's angular nose and pointed chin. Her hair is frizzy and
pulled back in her signature clump at the nape of her neck, held by a

scrunchie. It's just the easiest way she's found to handle it. And then there is the scar above her left eye, which she got from falling out of a tree a few years back. Mom and Uncle Jim had to rush her to the ER, where she got six stitches.

I am Erin, I say in my head, to the girl with the angular nose, and the frizzy hair that is a mystery to me, and the scar above her left eye. The girl who is staring back at me questioningly in the mirror. *And I am real.* Her hands grip the sides of the sink tighter and her stomach begins to swirl. *No,* she tells her brain and her stomach. *It's okay. Let's not do this now.* But it's already too late, I can feel the old, familiar fear on the other side of the door inside me, the one that is usually chained shut when I am lying in bed at night and my mind races—the door I either studiously ignore or nonchalantly walk past in daily life. She hates that door with everything in her. Hates its ability to knock her over when she usually has everything in control. Hates its audacity to exist. And now it is flung wide open, the fear leaping out of her in the form of questions she can't answer, that no one could: *You are not real. Because if you were real, who is saying this right now? Who is listening? And what is this "world" you think is so "real" anyway? What if it's all just a figment of your imagination? What if you're a robot and someone else is controlling you, controlling even these thoughts?* "It's not true," I say to the mirror. And the girl in the mirror repeats them back. "It's not true!" she exclaims, because the thoughts aren't stopping now; in fact, they're getting louder, pounding the edges of her skull, flooding into her heart so fast that she feels she can't breathe, and she has to sit on the toilet. "This is real," I say to myself, my head between my legs. "This is all there is, and I am real." These are the words that make the fear move, that bring her back to herself again. They become ground, wall, sky, solid background within which she can exist. "This is all there is, and I am real," I repeat over and over again, until my breathing slows, and my mind feels empty, and the fear has crawled back behind the door. And then there is a sharp popping noise from the mirror, which startles me. I jerk my head up, and see a tiny sphere appear in the center of the mirror. It is white and spiraling bigger and bigger.

"Wha—"

I stand up and walk toward the mirror. My heart is beating in my ears again, and I rub my eyes. The spiral emits sparks and even a little heat, and there are wisps of violet and red at its core. Most of it is white, though, a silvery whiteness that is almost hypnotizing in its beauty.

"This is not real," I whisper, because I know it can't be. Maybe the fear opened some long-dormant part of my brain that is disconnected from this reality and hooked into another one. Maybe I really do need to be in a mental institution, as I've always feared.

Still, the girl is entranced, and can't seem to stop herself from getting as close to the spiral as possible. It is humming as it turns, a high-pitched sound that is almost electrical. She takes a deep breath, and looks into the circle folding back on itself. It's like there is this tunnel of light, and on the other side I see myself peering back at me. I mean . . . not myself, exactly, but someone who looks exactly like me. It's like she is me and she isn't. She is covered in dirt, and her *Star Wars* T-shirt is ripped in two places.

"Who's there?" I'm asking. "Who is that?"

She is sitting on the ground in some kind of woods, but I can barely make it out. It looks all hazy, and like the tunnel is falling in on itself. It seems like she hears me, because she reaches her hand toward me, toward the center of the pulsating spiral. And her hand, which I recognize as my own, actually reaches through to the other side, beyond the spiral and through the mirror. I gasp as it comes inches from my face. And then all at once, the spiral pops so loudly that I jump back. The hand vanishes, and the spiral whirls faster and faster, shrinking and jumping back, shrinking and jumping back, until finally, with a sizzle and a spray of sparks, it collapses to a dot and then is gone.

I blink. I reach out to where the spiral was only a moment before, but now it is just mirror.

I angrily pat all over the mirror. I have to pull my hands away fast, because the surface is hot. "What? Where did it go?" But the mirror is silent. It yields nothing.

"Come back!" I yell into it. "Come back!" But nothing happens; all she sees is her reflection yelling back at her.

THE TOOLS OF MAINSTREAM LITERARY FICTION are inadequate for investigating my questions. You can get to the edges of them, but not inside them. For that, you need a wormhole. And multiple timelines. Perhaps a doppelgänger. For me, these are not manufactured literary devices. They are not lies. And yet, they absolutely are manufactured literary devices. And yes, they are lies. But only insofar as our manufactured birth certificates are lies. And the stories we were told as children by our loving parents about being given up because we were "special" are lies. Which is the lie: that my white birth mother knew my Black birth father just a little, and projected racist fears of predatory Black men onto him when she learned I was searching for him (before I found out he had died many years before)? Or that she was trying to protect me? Which is true? That I would have been loved but not cared for as well by my birth mother as by my solidly middle-class adoptive family? That my birth mother was not in a position to be a "good mother" to me, so she "did the right thing" by giving me up? Or that there is no right thing when it comes to cleaving the tie between mother and child?

What has become of the other me living out that first timeline, with my birth mother? How are you, Erin Powers? Who was that girl, and who is she now? I have never seen her, and yet I see her every day. Walking my dog, she passes me, her hair a little longer, a little frizzier, her eyes downcast. Leaving the grocery store, I see her smoking languidly on the steps, her Doc Martens scarred with red paint and glittery silver laces. She is funny, but reticent. She watches, but does not reveal. She holds her stories tightly. And like me, she knows that the truth is a slippery thing—that it can float in and out of what we accept as "real" in an instant. She could step through a wormhole at any minute, and she could be me, running a cross-country race at the high school, leaning into my Blackness in my twenties, and furiously trying to translate everything into words in my thirties. We could bump into each other on the way to meet our birth father, who neither of us actually met. All of it, all the possible *us*'s, exist without explanation, answer, or resolution. Just like our stories.

I am starving to know more.

Erin Powers is ten.

"HOW ARE YOU, Peanut Brittle?" Uncle Jim exclaims, taking Erin in his arms and spinning her around. It's Sunday dinner a few months later. Aunt Bridget, Aunt Kathleen, Grandma, Uncle Jim and his girl-friend, Susan, and a whole mess of cousins fill Grandma Powers' house.

Erin squeals happily and stretches her legs as far as they can go. She loves the way the air slices her calves as she whips around. "I'm good, good, goooooooodddddddd," she says.

Uncle Jim whips her around one more time before setting her down. Susan looks on, bemused, from a chair in the living room.

"More! More!" Erin tells him, her feet solidly planted on the ground again.

Uncle Jim laughs, reaching for his pack of cigarettes. "Sorry, cutie pie. Your uncle is getting old over here, and you are getting *big*." He pants dramatically. "I can't keep up. Gotta rest."

Erin puts a hand on her hip, playing along. "What, you gonna be in the old folks' home soon, or something? You're the baby, after all. And the only boy. You should be ready to lift a building if necessary. And I am waaaaayyy lighter than a building!"

Uncle Jim almost chokes on his cigarette. "That so, Peanut Brittle?" They are both laughing now.

Uncle Jim is Erin's favorite uncle, and the feeling seems mutual. *He adores that child. Would spoil her rotten if we let him. Needs a child of his own . . . Why can't he just marry Susan already?* Mom and the aunts whisper these things while huddled in corners, when they think he isn't listening.

"Yes, that is so, Rick Hunter," Erin says playfully. Rick Hunter is the ace pilot on *Robotech*. Uncle Jim looks nothing like him, but Erin doesn't care. Erin often imagines that she is Rick when she is day-dreaming, but when she is around Uncle Jim, she happily maps this dream on to him.

"Well, if I really *were* a Robotech warrior, I could maybe go into Battloid mode and lift you—no, make that throw you—across the room to your mother." Uncle Jim gestures dramatically at Mom, who is mixing drinks for dinner—and testing them as she goes along.

Erin's eyes grow wide. "You know about Battloid mode?"

Uncle Jim nods while lighting another cigarette. He winks at Susan, then turns his attention back to Erin. "I made Aunt Susan watch it with me the other day. Sounded interesting, the way you talk it up so much. Made me wanna be a Veritech pilot, myself."

Erin laughs, and hugs him hard. Everyone else thinks *Robotech* is just weird—even Essie. But it is about saving humanity and being a hero. And the one thing Erin has always known is that she is a hero. "We could do it together," she says, looking up through his thick glasses and into his cloudy gray eyes.

Uncle Jim hugs her back, squeezing her rail-thin shoulders. "Still not enough meat on your bones, though."

Erin groans. I hate this part.

"You sure your mom's feeding you enough over there?" Uncle Jim says this to me, but loud enough for Mom to hear.

I have always been "slight," as Grandma would say, always well under the standard weight for my age. I am tall and angular, with bird-like arms and legs, and knobby knees that stick out of every skirt and pair of shorts I wear. But I am also surprisingly strong and nimble, and can beat most of the boys in class at sprints. Still, it is not uncommon for adults and kids to look at me askance and ask if I eat. Both Mom and I have grown tired of it.

"Don't start, Jimmy," Mom says, right on cue.

"I'm just checking to make sure my number-one niece is eating all her fruits and vegetables," he says. "You know that's my job, Pat. No offense."

Uncle Jim pulls on one of Erin's frizzy curls affectionately. "Are you eating all your fruits and veggies, Peanut?"

I nod vigorously.

"None taken," Mom says. Her tone is neither icy nor warm.

Last winter, Uncle Jim and Susan brought over groceries every week, after they watched me stuff enormous spoonfuls of food into my mouth at Sunday dinner. Later I confessed that I hadn't eaten anything since the day before. Mom sat sullen at the table, arms crossed, as they dropped things off. But she always thanked them. And after they left, she unpacked all the bread, milk, eggs, peanut butter, meat, cookies, chips, cheese, apples, oranges, green beans, and carrots they brought us, and let me feast on whatever I wanted.

"Time to eat!" Aunt Kathleen says brightly. She is a full-fledged nurse, not a nursing assistant like Mom. She is still dressed in her scrubs from her morning shift and looks tired. She works in the pediatric ward, which Mom says is much better on your body than the cardiac ward, where she is. *Nursing runs in the family,* Mom and her sisters always say. *Watch out! You will probably be a nurse, too,* they tell me, simultaneously laughing and shaking their heads. I just frown when they say this. *Oh, you wait and see,* they say. *That's what we said, too.* But I know I won't be like them.

We sit down at Grandma Powers' huge dinner table, where a pot roast, mashed potatoes, gravy, green beans, salad, rolls, and squash make a delicious-smelling spread. I am excited about everything except the squash.

I sit next to my cousin Paul, Aunt Bridget's son, who is fifteen, and across from Uncle Jim, who looks as ready to eat as I am.

"Bless us, O Lord, and these Thy gifts, which we are about to receive, from Thy bounty, through Christ, Our Lord. Amen," says Mom, her voice hoarse and tired as usual.

I close my eyes during the grace, but for an instant as I open them, I think I see a young woman—maybe twenty or so—seated beside Mom. Her hands are clasped in prayer, her forehead bowed. She has very short hair, almost down to her scalp, actually, and her skin is the same color as mine. The very same light brown with yellow undertones. When the prayer ends, she opens her eyes, and I swear for a minute that it's my eyes I'm looking at across the table. I blink, and my stomach drops in panic. *Please, let there be no spiral. Please, let there be no spiral!* When I blink again, she is gone.

"Erin?" Uncle Jim asks, across the table.

Everyone has begun serving themselves, passing the food and taking portions.

Erin stares at him, confused for a moment. "Uncle Jim," she says slowly, coming back to herself.

"Are you okay, honey?" he asks. He reaches for her hand across the table.

Erin pulls it away quickly, resting it on her lap. "Fine," she says, smiling.

Uncle Jim lets out a short, uncomfortable laugh. "You sure, honey?" he asks. "Because you don't look okay at all. You look like you've seen a ghost . . . Doesn't she look pale, Pat?"

Mom is whispering something to Aunt Bridget. The two of them are giggling.

Uncle Jim sighs. The pot roast, mashed potatoes, and gravy are stopped with him, but he doesn't even care, he's so distracted. "Pat!" he says impatiently.

"What?" she asks crossly, before she catches herself. "What?" she asks again, in a nicer tone.

"Your daughter," says Uncle Jim. "Doesn't she look pale to you?"

Mom laughs, unable to stop herself. "Pale? Jimmy, what's gotten into you? Erin is the last person in the family anyone would describe as pale."

Everyone at the table, except for Grandma and Uncle Jim, laughs at that. I don't think it's a funny joke at all, the fact that I am the only Black person at the table. In fact, my mother saying so like that has created a growing hole in my stomach. And I think I see a glimmering image of the twenty-year-old lady across the table, shaking her head at the comment, too.

"That's enough, Pat," Grandma says softly.

Mom gets a hold of herself, and everyone quiets down quickly.

Grandma lifts a forkful of beef into her mouth, chews for a moment, then swallows. "The roast is delicious, isn't it?"

Everyone murmurs in agreement around the table. No one disputes what Grandma says, and if she asks you to do something, you do it. I love coming over to her house, because she is the one person Mom will listen to. Sometimes.

For a while, the only sound in the room is of silverware clinking, and glasses being lifted up and set back down. I can focus on the succulent juice of the meat, the tangy bite of the salad dressing.

"Did anyone see all that construction going on over on Twelve, at Burrstone?" Aunt Bridget asks after a moment. She has Mom's same dirty blond hair, the same rounded shoulders, thick with tension.

Aunt Kathleen groans. "God, that set me way back this morning. I was fifteen minutes late to my shift!"

Grandma nods. "Yes, I think they plan to resurface that whole portion, all the way up to Five."

A collective groan follows, around the table.

"Of course that'll take them months to finish," says Uncle Jim.

"And when it's done, it won't be done right," says Susan.

"It's never done right," says Aunt Kathleen.

"Because they don't know how to do it right, those people," says Mom. "What they know how to do right is breed like rabbits."

I look up from cutting my meat, to see all of the grown-ups, including Uncle Jim, nodding in agreement.

"Mexicans damn near everywhere now," says Bridget.

My skin pricks. It feels translucent.

"Bridget," says Grandma. "Don't swear at the dinner table."

Bridget smiles at Grandma, across the room. "Sorry, Mom."

Later, back at home, the girl's mother tucks her in. She is sweaty and sticky from all her exertions and from devouring the German chocolate cake her grandmother made for dessert, but she is also sated. Her stomach is full, and her eyes are droopy. But she still wants the ritual of story her mother bestows upon her every night.

"'So, he's taken her with him up to his place in Scotland,'" the girl's mother reads, seated on the edge of her bed. They have been reading *Lassie Come-Home* for the past week, despite the demands of the narrator's accent and the fact that it makes the girl's request for a dog even more prominent.

"What? Scotland?" the girl says sleepily. "How could they?"

Her mother nods demurely and continues reading about how the dog will be taken away, back to Scotland, never to return to Yorkshire.

"'So there it is, and put it in thy pipe and smoke it,'" her mother reads.

"No," the girl protests. But there is no energy behind it. Sleep is slowly taking her.

Her mother reads on, undeterred. "'Now what can't be helped in this life must be endured, Joe lad. So bide it like a man, and let's never say another word about it as long as we live—especially in front o' thy mother.' "

The girl frowns, and stirs under her covers. "It's not fair," she says crossly.

Her mother nods. "It's not fair," she agrees. She goes back to the book, reading a passage about stumbling over a difficult path through rocky crags over something called a moor. All along, the child's father is silent, an empty pipe between his lips, only speaking when they reach the village: " 'Just afore we go in, Joe,' he said, 'I want thee to think on thy mother. Tha's growing up, and tha must try to be like a man wit' her and understand her.' "

Even though she is half-asleep, the girl laughs. "What does that mean? Be a man? He's trying to say that he shouldn't care that his dog is gone now? And his mother shouldn't, either?"

Mom sighs, and closes the book. "I think that's enough for tonight. We'll read more tomorrow, and you can find out."

The girl shakes her head. "Grown-ups are weird."

Her mother stands up, and pulls the girl's blankets to her chin, tightly. Then she kisses her on the forehead. The smell of nicotine wafts from her hair to the girl's nose, comforting in its familiarity. This is the one unabashed moment, the one gesture of tenderness that both of them look forward to each day. "Yes, they are."

The girl harrumphs. "Yes, *we* are."

Her mother looks at her in confusion.

"You're an adult, Mom," the girl says, raising an eyebrow.

Her mother chuckles. "Yeah, I forget that sometimes."

The girl looks at her mother strangely, getting the courage to ask her a question she has been turning over in her mind lately. "My father," she asks softly. "Was he like Joe's father?"

"What?"

The girl sits up in her bed, now fully awake. "My father. You never talk about him . . . But was he always saying things like, 'Bide it like a man,' and 'What can't be helped in this life must be endured'? Like giving advice to you that you didn't want to take? Trying to be a man or whatever. I know you said he was a lot older than you . . ."

My mother's eyes go wide. Of course, I had asked questions here and there throughout the years, but I'd never gotten a complete story. Never an accounting of *why*. My mother had to know it would come someday, the demand to make a narrative out of what stubbornly remain just pieces, images, from the distant past. But is this really that day? She sits back down on my bed, sighing. Her hands shake a bit. "You should know whatever you want about him." She looks away, to the Mickey Mouse curtains she found at Goodwill for my windows.

I tap my mother's hand urgently. "But I want to know everything," she says. "Everything, Mom."

The girl's mother stands up, suddenly, angry. "Well, I don't know everything, Erin," she says crossly. "In fact, I only know a little. A very little."

Then she looks back at her fierce daughter's yearning, sleepy eyes, and something in her yields. "Okay, this is what I know." She sits down beside Erin on the bed, and gingerly takes her hand. "We met at a disco, at the airport base not far from here." Her brow furrows. "He was in the air force. We talked about Detroit and music. We were both into Dylan, and Joan Baez . . ." Erin's mother smiles.

"Is he still there? At the airport base?" her daughter asks anxiously.

Her mother shakes her head. "No, I'm sure he's moved on."

Her daughter cocks her head to the side, unconvinced. "Are you positive?"

Her mother nods vigorously. "Absolutely, one hundred percent positive."

The girl sighs, visibly disappointed. "Okay, Mom," the girl says, staring at her expectantly. "Go on."

"He had a steel guitar," she says. "I would write lyrics, and we would sing together."

Her daughter laughs. "Really? You wrote lyrics?"

"Yup."

Erin is not convinced. "Really? You?"

Her mother crosses her arms in front of her chest. "Yes, really. Me. Is that so hard to believe?"

Her daughter does not answer, but just continues to look at her incredulously.

"*When the night rains, the moon will hold sway,*" she sings softly.

Her daughter claps in delight. "What? Was that one of the songs?"

My mother shakes her head.

"Is it? Is it?" Her daughter pulls on her arm playfully. "Sing more, Mom! Sing more."

She shakes her daughter's arm off. "I can't. That's all I remember."

Her daughter takes one hand in the other, sitting up straight on the bed. It is a posture she assumes when she feels she needs to be resolute, firm. And also when she is disappointed. "Oh," she says.

"He had a blue Olds 442, and he taught me how to drive stick shift on it," she says. "I remember sitting there cross-legged on the floor at a friend's apartment when I told him I was pregnant with you. And the first thing he said is that we should get married. And my stomach was churning in knots because I knew I couldn't do it. I mean, I knew I could get out of a marriage if I had to, but I couldn't do that to a child."

"Do what to a child?" the girl asks. She feels so awake now. More awake than she can remember feeling in a very long time.

My mother, Patricia Powers, blinks. "Put a child in an unsafe situation."

I am more confused than ever. "He was dangerous?"

"He . . . wasn't stable, Erin," she says quietly. "He wouldn't have known how to be around a child."

I think of Uncle Jim suddenly and his bright red Olds 442.

Then I glare at her. "How would you know?" She picks at the comforter. The girl that I am is irritated. This isn't how I thought the talk would go.

"Bedtime," the woman who is my mother says suddenly, and stands up. Then she flicks off the light and stomps out of the room.

"Mom! Come on," I plead. But I know it is pointless. Besides, sleep is becoming increasingly difficult to resist. She closes her eyes and wills the conversation to memory before drifting off.

Memory

"Shannon, did Patricia tell you your father had an Olds 442?"

"No. Made that up. I seem to remember her telling me he had some kind of fancy car that he would drive them around in."

They met at a disco — airport base in NY (Rome), while he was in airforce. Talked @ Detroit & music (Dylan, Joan Baez, etc.).

He had a steel guitar. She would write lyrics & they would sing together. He taught her to drive stick shift — red sports car (same as Uncle Denny...).

"I remember sitting there cross-legged on the floor at a friend's apt. when I told him I was pregnant. And the first thing out of his mouth was that we should get married. And my stomach churning in knots because I knew I couldn't do it. I mean, I knew I could get out of a marriage if I had to, but I couldn't do that to a child."

From notes on a conversation with Patricia in 1994.

Boisey Collins Jr. is thirty-four.

WHEN HE HEARS THE TRANSMISSION go out again, he pulls off to the side of the Bayshore Freeway. The Oldsmobile 442 was never meant to be a reliable car. My father bought it because of its sheer brawn and audacious bright red sheen. And because his friend Teddy was willing to sell it to him for his last thousand bucks. Ten years old and mostly filled with half-price replacement parts, the car chugs along well enough. Until it doesn't, and my father has to pull out his bag of fix-it tricks he perfected in his short-lived Air Force days.

"Motherfucker," he says, in the slow drawl that only a Black man can use to massage the expletive.

The car shudders one last time before he turns off the engine. It has been increasingly difficult to get it to stay in gear, but he was hoping it could last at least another week, until he's sure to get that windfall from the appliance scam.

"Goddamnit!" He feels better the louder he cusses, so he says it again, and then hits the steering wheel a few times for good measure. Why is everything going so completely to shit lately? He had a plan, a good one. Harry would lift the product, he and Jorge would deliver it to Francie for the resale, and everyone would get paid and laid, as they say. But Harry had had some hiccups lifting the product, Jorge was busy on another gig until Tuesday, and Francie had to temporarily close down shop since the pigs had been sniffing around lately. *Story of my goddamn life,* my father thinks to himself. Then he gets out of the car and slams the door so hard he thinks for a moment he has broken the door handle again. But no, when he jiggles it, he finds that he can still open the door. *Get ahold of yourself, man,* he says as cars whiz past. *This ain't that bad, really. You been through plenty worse.* Hands shaking, he takes out his pack of cigarettes and his lighter. The memories will come now, not all of them, he prays, but plenty to make his brain feel broken, his heart overwhelmed. His parents in one of their frequent arguments, screaming, while he hides under the kitchen table alone, just a toddler. His sister Delphine calling for him to help her at fourteen when two of the older dudes in his crew dragged her inside the shed. His first snort of coke, how it raced through his veins and woke up every single cell. And later, his first hit of heroin, dulling the seemingly ever-present pain. The women, all of the women—many of them kind, some of them not— whom he could never seem to give what they wanted.

My father's hands are shaking hard now, as he works to plug the avalanche of memories falling through his body. Although his thumb will not be still, he somehow manages to get it to flick the lighter, and then slowly moves his head, and the cigarette toward the flame. It takes, and he breathes in the sweet relief of nicotine, which he knows will help get the memories moving and unstuck from all the hiding places inside him. *My damn brain,* he thinks. *If I could just get it to shut the fuck up!* But then, his brain is what got him into the Air Force in the first place. *You the smart one in this family, Junior,* his father used to tell him. *Don't waste it.* My father takes another drag and blows the smoke out ruefully. *But you did, didn't you?* He turns around, facing the highway now, letting the shock of the speeding passing cars overwhelm his senses. Sometimes, that is enough to get his brain out of the stuck place. And then, out of nowhere it seems, a miracle: A song appears in his mind. The lyrics are something about moving like God's immaculate machine. My father frowns. He can't actually place the song, although he knows it's Paul Simon. Where has he heard this? How does he know it, even?

"'One-Trick Pony,'" I say, suddenly beside him.

My father jumps. "Who—?" He glances around himself, trying to discover where I've come from, I suppose.

I shrug. He of all people should know the answer to that question. "From Paul Simon's album."

My father peers at me incredulously, taking in my frizzy fourth-grade afro, my hand-me-down pink-and-gray shorts and faded *Star Wars* T-shirt. "Who the hell are you? How did you get here? Where are your parents?"

I laugh, delighted at this line of questioning. There is something familiar about his voice. Some quality I can't quite pinpoint. "I'm Shannon," I say. "And my parents aren't worried. They're nearby."

He takes a step back from me then, clearly disturbed. He looks around again, taking in the wide expanse of the four-lane highway, the boxy office buildings that dot the landscape. "I don't see them anywhere," he says. Then he shakes his head. "And I don't understand. How'd you . . . I wasn't singing out loud, was I? No, I wasn't. How'd you know . . . ?"

I step as close to him as I can, so that our hands are almost touching. ". . . what song was in your head? Because I heard it, too. I mean, I hear it. My dad, I mean my *other* dad, plays it all the time. In Ann Arbor. Me and my brothers love it. We even made a dance to it. Want to see?"

My father shakes his head slowly. "No."

I shuffle my gangly legs and sing a few lyrics as best I can. "Something like that." I frown. "But I can't remember it very well right now for some reason. I think it's because . . . I'm not supposed to be here."

This piques my father's interest. "What do you mean?"

I cross my arms. "I don't know. I just know that the timelines got botched. Then pieces and people from one place get put in another, and the strangest things . . ." I cannot finish my sentence because I feel a ripple like electricity shock through me.

"Oh my God!" my father is screaming. "What the fuck is going on? What was that?"

I fall to the ground once the ripple has passed. I feel exhausted, like someone has pushed all the air out of me. "What did you see?"

He is pulling at the ends of his shirt one minute, and then gesticulating wildly the next. "You were like, *invisible* or something! Like, see-through. It was some *Star Wars* shit or something. I don't know . . . Like an electrical wave moved through you. Almost as if you were fading out of here . . ."

". . . and into somewhere else," I say, finally catching my breath. "I think my time here is almost up."

He crouches down, so that he is almost on the ground with me. "Are you okay?" His hand reaches out to touch my back, but when it makes contact, another electrical ripple surges through me, and I can see the tangle of trees in the woods behind our house on Terhune in Ann Arbor for a moment, before I am ripped back to him. I gasp at the raw smack of the ground, at the shock of embodiment.

"Oh my God!" he exclaims, a spark ripping through my arm and singeing his own.

I shake my head, knowing somehow that this is the last thing I will say to him before I go. "Your brain is fine, Dad. You gave it to me, too."

He almost leaps away from me then, onto the highway itself.

"Watch out!" I yell as a truck barrels dangerously close to him. The driver honks his horn, and my father, Boisey Collins Jr., runs back beside me. Except I am no longer there. I am back home already.

Speculation

THE BAYSHORE FREEWAY is a stretch of U.S. Route 101 near San Francisco. I have never been on the Bayshore Freeway, but California is a place I often fantasize about visiting with my son and daughter when it's winter in Minnesota and the whole world is cold and white. I wonder if Erin Powers would ever have seen the Bayshore Freeway by the time she turned forty-eight. No one knows if Boisey Collins Jr. was actually ever on the Bayshore Freeway, but we do know that he never turned forty-eight.

Shannon Gibney is forty-four.

"BOISEY! TIME TO GO!"

It is five minutes to eight, and lightly snowing outside. My son is playing quietly with his Legos on the living room floor, as he does most school-day mornings after he has completed his morning routine.

Phone in my hand, I scroll through the weather report for the day: ten o'clock, twenty-two degrees, a little more snow; eleven o'clock, same temperature, a snow shower predicted. "Snow pants on, boots on, hat on," I tell Boisey.

I hear the sounds of an eight-year-old blasting a Lego cruiser out of an imaginary sky with a robot cannon and shake my head. Most of my friends' kids cannot get ready to go in under a half hour in the morning, but my son consistently does it in fifteen minutes—quite a feat. And yet, every day it is a battle to pull him away from that imaginary world he can magically inhabit at a moment's notice, and get back into this real one, with school and buses and mothers who want you to do things.

"If you don't get to it now, you will miss the bus," I say.

"Boom! Ahhhhh! The hangar is exploded." He holds the cruiser at a forty-five-degree angle to the ground, where a Black Panther action figure, twice the size of the cruiser, stands, ready to catch it. "Wakanda forever, my friends! I have you."

Agitated, I grab Boisey's snow pants from the hanger and throw them to him. "On. Now," I say, in my sternest voice.

He glances at me out of the side of his eye, probably trying to gauge how serious my tone is.

"Or no TV," I say.

It works, because he sets the toys down and reluctantly pulls on each leg of the snow pants. As he does, I carefully place his hat on his head so that it covers his ears. Then I grab his winter coat from the front, and shrug it over the wide shoulders he has had since birth. He leans over, all his attention on the front zipper. I remember how much work just getting the zipper to catch was at six and well into seven, so it seems fairly miraculous that he can maneuver it all so easily now. Next, we put on a worn-down winter boot, and hunt around our modest and always cluttered living room for the other one. We find it in one of the overflowing buckets of toys that he and his four-year-old sister have strewn across the floor.

"How did it get over here?" he asks me, and then grabs my shoulder to steady himself while he puts it on. Even though there is still far too much touching and hanging over my neck and insisting on sleeping in my bed after nightmares and kicking me while falling asleep and waking up—even though my body is still not mine—I do relish these small moments of physical support I can give him. The knowledge that his mother is steady, and omnipresent.

"You tell me," I say, chuckling.

"Mawe," he says wryly, invoking his sister. She is splayed out unconscious on the bed, in the other room.

"Hmm," I say, rummaging through the disorganized basket of gloves and hats and scarves in front of us. "She's an easy target." I pull out a worn pair of gray ski gloves, ripped on one side, but serviceable. I regard it as a miracle that I have been able to find a matching pair of anything.

I rub some lotion on his dry hands, and he shudders from its coldness. His hands are chestnut brown, due to his Liberian father's dark skin. I much prefer it to the sallow yellow color my skin turns in winter.

"Sorry," I say, and rub harder to create friction.

He pulls away after I have only rubbed in half of what I have on my hands. "I'm fine," he says, and I sigh. One battle at a time.

I grab his bright green backpack from the corner, and then it's one arm in through the strap and then the other.

"What are we forgetting?" I ask, my brain still foggy from sleep. There are so many things to remember getting both children out the door in the morning. Most days I am shocked that it happens at all.

He shrugs, walking to the door.

"Glasses!" I exclaim. Then I unzip his backpack, extract the glasses case, and his small, child-sized green-rimmed glasses. He has almost no correction in one eye, and just a slight correction in the other, so he almost doesn't need them. Almost.

When I slip the glasses on, he looks so much older: twelve or eleven to his actual eight. So studious, so caring, so gentle and innocent. Everything Black boys are assumed not to be in this country. And you can still see the glow of his inquisitive brown eyes behind the lenses. His father may have gifted him the elegant almond shape of his eyes, but their glow and intensity are all mine. This is the daily satisfaction of finally having a family that looks like me. And of not carrying Blackness alone.

"Have a good day, honey," I say, opening the door. The cold blasts us and we brace, me against the doorframe, he against his backpack straps.

He nods, and then he is off, down the road and then to the right and down another one, to the corner where the bus will pick him up in approximately six minutes. I watch the permanent-marker strip of "Boisey Corvah" written across the top of his backpack get smaller and smaller, wondering if my birth father or my uncle or my grandfather before them could ever have imagined a child so magical, so free from the burdens that ground them down, bearing their name so lightly.

Boisey Collins Jr.

Shannon Gibney.

Boisey Corvah.

Shannon Gibney is nineteen.

"You spoke to me so many years ago when I chose to listen to your yearning to be in this world. (it was actually a scream to me)"

you spoke to me so many years ago when I chose to listen to your yearning to be in this world. (it was actually a scream to me)

this is happening for a reason. we both are meant to learn something here. we both are teachers too, according to principles of learning theory, (Based on Nursing Research), ~~teacher~~ teaching will occur only when the teacher is open to learning ... (Based on 14 principles of learning theory).

   I look forward to your visit - I hope we can go to Bookstore together. one day too I would love to show you and Eric →

Patricia Powers is nineteen.
Erin Powers and Shannon Gibney are not yet.

"YOU'RE DOING GREAT, Patricia!"

She feels like she has been pushing all night, but in reality, it has only been two and a half hours. It's like someone has run a truck over and through her body, and left little more than her mouth to howl about it all, and presumably, a stubborn baby still lodged firmly between her pelvic bones.

"Fuck!" she roars as another contraction almost obliterates her with its searing pain.

"This baby is almost here!" This from the doc who's been anxiously peering into her vagina for the past hour. In the last fifteen minutes, he's been fumbling with forceps down there, the cold metal making her jump as he inserted them without warning. She would kick him in the face if she could maneuver her feet out of the stirrups. They've had her hooked up to this hospital bed since she was admitted, and it's past time to get her out. Her sister, Mary Sheila, asked the staff three times if she could walk around, that she was sure her sister would handle contractions better with movement, but they just shook their heads and mumbled something about hospital protocol.

"Okay, it's crowning!" the doctor exclaims as a new jolt of pain, sharper than any of the contractions, hits her vagina. "I can see the head. It's coming through, it's coming through."

My mother can barely keep herself from exploding into a million different pieces as I am reluctantly pulled by the steel blades of metal forceps into the cold, bright world. I have pushed myself through the birth canal over thirteen hours, and I am hungry and exhausted. I did not want to come here yet. I wanted to be safe and warm inside her uterus, instead. Even in its beauty, I already know that the world will be difficult. This is knowledge she has communicated to me, just as she's shared her own blood with me.

Patricia screams, and finally the baby is in the hands of the nurse, cradling its tiny bottom and long little legs.

I stare at the bright lights everywhere around me. They are too much; I want them to go away. I begin to shiver, and make a small sucking noise with my mouth.

A nurse clamps and then cuts the umbilical cord.

The pain is finally over, and Patricia can almost breathe again. The pressure has been relieved, and the doctor tells her they just have to wait for the placenta. "Shouldn't be long at all now," he says, resting his old, speckled hand on her arm. He pats her like a dog.

"What . . . Where is it?" my mother says. "Is it okay?"

"Hmm, what now?" the doctor says, sticking his crusty white face in hers.

"My baby," she says. What is wrong with these people? "My baby. Where is it?"

"She's right here," the nurse says from across the room.

I watch Patricia attempt to lift herself up onto her elbows. "She's . . . It's a she?" she asks. I remember she did not want to talk to one more doctor or pay one more hospital bill, so she never got an ultrasound to see the sex of the baby. All indications were that it was—I was—a healthy, normal pregnancy all the way through, except for being born of an unwed mother, of course.

I wonder what she thinks now that she knows I am a girl.

The nurse looks embarrassed, across the room. She meets the doctor's eyes, and with some trepidation, nods. "Congratulations," she says quietly. "You have a healthy baby girl." Then her face reddens, and she shakes her head. "I mean, you gave *birth* to a healthy baby girl. She's not yours, of course . . ."

"Bring her. Bring her to me."

The nurse freezes, and the doctor shakes his head at her solemnly. Then he turns to our mother. "That's not a good idea," he says gravely. He takes our mother's hand. "It's not good for either of you to get attached."

She shakes him off, eyes still trained on me. "That's my baby," she says. "That's my daughter."

We recognize her voice, and we gurgle. We are still hungry. Also, cold.

The doctor frowns. "She's not actually—"

"Goddamnit!" our mother yells. "I just gave birth to her, for Christsakes. She's my flesh and blood. I at least deserve to see her!"

"Ms. Powers, I'm afraid we can't do that," the doctor says in even tones, shooing the nurse with the baby out of the room. "You may have given birth to her, but legally, now, you are not her mother."

We are already out of the room, the nurse holding us tight to her chest as she walks quickly down the hall. We register my mother's sobs, and they lodge permanently at the base of our spine, where we will carry them always.

THE LITERATURE OF ADOPTION IS A FICTIONAL GENRE IN ITSELF.
Adoptees know it to be generally as fantastical as any space opera—and just as entertaining to the masses.

Every story must begin with the vulnerable but good-hearted poor birth mother who loves her baby very much but cannot take care of it (the birth father is always conspicuously absent in these narratives). There is a kindly, upper-middle-class, usually white couple who desperately wants a child, and have pursued all avenues in order to get one (if the couple is adopting internationally, they are in a rich country in the Global North, and have spent years on various lists, waiting for an available child, many times spending thousands of dollars). They fight, despite all odds, to build their family through adoption, in the process creating a healthy, happy, thriving child who eventually grows into a healthy, happy, thriving adult who has bonded perfectly with their new colorblind family. All this miraculous transformation from a poor, brown, cast-off orphan. *Love conquers all.*

Once the birth mother has given up the child, she is no longer part of the story.

Once the child is adopted, there is no talk of loss of first family, culture, language, or community. The adoption is simply a bureaucratic event that happened, and then is over.

Since the birth father was not part of the story from the beginning, he is not part of the adoptee's story as it progresses.

And if you ask about any of the particularities of this literature of adoption: who is adopting whom, from where to where, what are the racial dynamics of the transaction, the role that money plays, corruption, the trauma of removal, the burden of assimilation, you are branded *an angry and mal-adjusted adoptee.*

When most of the literature written about a marginalized group of people comes from white adoptive parents who are psychologists, sociologists, creative writers, and professors who don't identify themselves as adoptive parents in their "objective" work, what other possible outcome could there be?

This is how I came to understand epistemological violence.

In my body.

From a letter Patricia sent my mom, date unknown (2010s?).

PATRICIA AND I HAD BEEN ESTRANGED FOR YEARS BY THIS TIME, but she had met my parents during my college graduation in 1997 and still kept in touch.

Dear Sue,

[. . .] Thank-you for recognizing my vulnerability back when I was pregnant with Shannon. I try to accept her anger, her disappointments in me. I was so afraid back then, so lost when I realized I was pregnant. My whole lifestyle at that time was lost. I even went so far as to sign-up for an abortion. (It was the 1st year after Roe vs. Wade)—the political powers of the day wanted the numbers up there. When I reported for my appointment, I told the nurse I couldn't go through with it. She tried to talk me into it, as did a couple of my friends. Shannon's father wanted to marry me. He too was a lost soul. I told him no, that we would ruin a child. Anyway, the nurse at the clinic persisted and wanted to know why I wouldn't go through with it. I told her that I felt this life within me was screaming to be born. I had no choice but to listen. She is still screaming to live, to become the woman she will be. You have been the force of life and love for her. I can't even begin to thank you and tell you how grateful I am that you and Jim gave her all the gifts of life and love. You are the kinds of people the world needs right now—and so does Shannon . . .

Sorry for the length of this.

Patricia

☒ HEINEMANN

Italia

Via Speranza 27
40068 San Lazzaro di S. BOLOGNA
Tel. 051/454570 · Fax 051/454804

-3-

I did not intend this should be so long.

Thank you for recognizing my vulnerability back when I was pregnant c̄ Shannon. I try to accept her anger, her disappointments in me. I was so afraid back then, so lost when I realized I was pregnant. My whole lifestyle at that time was lost. I even went so far as to sign-up for an abortion. (It was the 1st year after Roe vs. Wade) -- the political powers of the day wanted the numbers up there. When I reported

→

Contradiction

THIS IS A TRANSCRIPT OF A STORY told by my mother, Sue Gibney, gathered on November 14, 2019.

SHANNON GIBNEY: *So tell me what you remember about Mary Sheila and St. John's Catholic Church.*

SUSAN GIBNEY: *When we met and visited with Patricia's sister Mary Sheila when you were around twenty-one, she told us the story—or the backstory—of how you came to be born in Michigan.*

What she said was that when Patricia was pregnant in Utica, Mary Sheila brought her to the convent where she was living. At that point, she was still a nun. She brought Patricia to take care of her, and keep an eye on her, because Patricia had had some history that worried Mary Sheila. And to keep her healthy and safe during her pregnancy. So, you were living in the convent at St. John the Baptist Church in Ypsilanti, Michigan . . . I mean, you were there, in your mom, Patricia. And then you were born at St. Joseph Hospital, which is now in Ypsilanti. At the time, it was in Ann Arbor.

Mary Sheila told me that Patricia kept you with her for a couple of days after.

SHANNON: *What? 'Cause they never let . . . That's the whole thing about bonding . . . especially in that time. I mean, more in the '50s and '60s . . .*

SUSAN: *Mary Sheila saw it as unusual. And I certainly saw it as unusual. But that's what Mary Sheila said. And she even told me that Patricia tried to breastfeed you during that time that you were with her. And she thought that that was important for you—as an educated kind of person, she knew psychologically the difficulty in placing a child for adoption. And what that could mean to Patricia, in feeling like she'd done something for you.*

IN THIS SPACE, in the space between the stories . . . in the space between what really happened, what could have happened, what almost happened, what did happen to another girl with another mother who relinquished her and another absent Black father . . . in this space is where we exist, where we have always existed. Where truth is born and exiled.

Patricia Powers is nineteen.
Erin Powers and Shannon Gibney are not yet.

"YOU'RE DOING GREAT, Patricia!"

She feels like she has been pushing all night, but in reality, it has only been two and a half hours. It's like someone has run a truck over and through her body, and left little more than her mouth to howl about it all, and presumably, a stubborn baby still lodged firmly between her pelvic bones.

"Fuck!" she roars as another contraction almost obliterates her with its searing pain.

"This baby is almost here!" This from the doc who's been anxiously peering into her vagina for the past hour. In the last fifteen minutes, he's been fumbling with forceps down there, the cold metal making her jump as he inserted them without warning. She would kick him in the face if she could maneuver her feet out of the stirrups. They've had her hooked up to this hospital bed since she was admitted, and it's past time to get her out. Her sister, Mary Sheila, asked the staff three times if she could walk around, that she was sure her sister would handle contractions better with movement, but they just shook their heads and mumbled something about hospital protocol.

"Okay, it's crowning!" the doctor exclaims as a new jolt of pain, sharper than any of the contractions, hits her vagina. "I can see the head. It's coming through, it's coming through."

My mother can barely keep herself from exploding into a million different pieces as I am reluctantly pulled by the steel blades of metal forceps into the cold, bright world. I have pushed myself through the birth canal over thirteen hours, and I am hungry and exhausted. I did not want to come here yet. I wanted to be safe and warm inside her uterus, instead. Even in its beauty, I already know that the world will be difficult. This is knowledge she has communicated to me, just as she's shared her own blood with me.

Patricia screams, and finally the baby is in the hands of the nurse, cradling its tiny bottom and long little legs.

I stare at the bright lights everywhere around me. They are too much; I want them to go away. I begin to shiver, and make a small sucking noise with my mouth.

A nurse clamps and then cuts the umbilical cord.

The pain is finally over, and Patricia can almost breathe again. The pressure has been relieved, and the doctor tells her they just have to wait for the placenta. "Shouldn't be long at all now," he says, resting his old, speckled hand on her arm. He pats her like a dog.

"What . . . Where is it?" my mother says. "Is it okay?"

"Hmm, what now?" the doctor says, sticking his crusty white face in hers.

"My baby," she says. What is wrong with these people? "My baby. Where is it?"

"She's right here," the nurse says from across the room.

I watch Patricia attempt to lift herself up onto her elbows. "She's . . . It's a she?" she asks. I remember she did not want to talk to one more doctor or pay one more hospital bill, so she never got an ultrasound to see the sex of the baby. All indications were that it was—I was—a healthy, normal pregnancy all the way through, except for being born of an unwed mother, of course.

I wonder what she thinks now that she knows I am a girl.

The nurse looks embarrassed, across the room. She meets the doctor's eyes, and with some trepidation, nods. "Congratulations," she says quietly. "You have a healthy baby girl." Then her face reddens, and she shakes her head. "I mean, you gave birth to a healthy baby girl. She's not yours, of course . . ."

"Bring her. Bring her to me."

The nurse freezes, and the doctor shakes his head at her solemnly. Then he turns to our mother. "That's not a good idea," he says gravely. He takes our mother's hand. "It's not good for either of you to get attached."

She shakes him off, eyes still trained on me. "That's my baby," she says. "That's my daughter."

We recognize her voice, and we gurgle. We are still hungry. Also, cold.

The doctor frowns. "She's not actually . . ."

"Goddamnit!" our mother yells. "I just gave birth to her, for Christsakes. She's my flesh and blood. I at least deserve to see her!"

"Ms. Powers, I'm afraid we can't do that," the doctor says in even tones, shooing the nurse with the baby out of the room. "You may have given *birth* to her, but legally, now, you are not her mother."

We are already out of the room, the nurse holding us tight to her chest as she walks quickly down the hall. We register my mother's sobs, and they lodge permanently at the base of our spine, where we will carry them always.

(THERE ARE SO MANY PARTS OF ME that must be written in strike-through.)

(And then rewritten.)

(And revised again.)

Non-Identifying Information

THIS IS THE STORY OF MY LIFE—or at least the story of my life as I came to know it. It was sent to me by the agency that facilitated my adoption, in answer to my request for "non-identifying information," or information that would not reveal the identity of my birth parents. I received it when I was nineteen.

Nothing has been omitted or changed.

Every time I read it, whether in 1994, 2003, or 2019, whether I am starting college and the same age as my birth mother when she gave me up, or I am thirty-two and wondering if I will ever have children of my own, I see a slightly different story, a loose narrative thread that has not yet been pulled, an opportunity to change the protagonist or rewrite the villain. It is a story (Patricia) mashed with a story (her parents and family), mashed with a story (me), mashed with a half-told story (Boisey). It is:

**THE DEFINITIVE ORIGIN STORY ACCORDING TO
THE STATE AND ITS CHILD WELFARE APPARATUS**

It is, like most stories, a projection of *me* according to *them*. Still, it remains one of the sole documents I have about the circumstances surrounding my birth and relinquishment. Most other adoptees I know, many of them internationally adopted from Korea, have close to nothing.

In the child welfare and social work context, "non-identifying information" includes the health, developmental, behavioral health, educational, and social histories of the adopted child and the child's parents and other biological relatives. Almost all states allow an adult adoptee access to non-identifying information about birth family, generally upon written request. The adoptee must be at least eighteen before they may retrieve this information. Indeed, access to one's own origin story is more closely guarded than admission to any movie.

Child and Family
Services of Michigan, Inc.

Post Office Box 348
Okemos, Michigan
48805

Ms. Shannon Gibney

**Child and Family
Services of Michigan, Inc.**

The Family . . .
our concern for
over 100 years.

2157 University Park Drive
Post Office Box 348
Okemos, Michigan
48805

517/349-6226

**Member:
Local United Ways**

Member of:
Child Welfare
League of America

Family Service America

Michigan Association
of Children's Alliances

Michigan Federation of Private
Child and Family Agencies

Accreditated by:*
Council on Accreditation
of Services for Families
and Children, Inc.

Member Agency
Locations:

Adrian*

Alpena

Battle Creek*

Holland*

Holt*

Howell

Jackson*

Kalamazoo*

Midland*

St. Joseph

Traverse City

August 24, 1994

Ms. Shannon Elaine Gibney

Dear Ms. Gibney:

This is in response to your phone call requesting information identifying your birth parents. The revised Michigan adoption law which became effective 9/10/80 established a procedure to be followed in response to such requests.

Enclosed is form DSS-1925 for you to complete and return to our office. This form will permit us to check with the Central Registry to see if either of your biological parents have filed a statement of consent to, or denial of, access. When we receive a reply from the Registry, you will be contacted. You will also receive a summary of the non-identifying information with that response. Also, enclosed is a pamphlet which describes the updated law and another form, DSS-1920 which you may or may not wish to sign and return. This authorization permits us to release your name and location if we are contacted by the birth family.

Our fee for accessing adoption records is $60.00. Payment should now be included with your written request for information. We are pleased to offer this service which is supported by donations and user fees.

If you have questions regarding the enclosed information, please do not hesitate to contact me at 1-800-878-6587.

Sincerely,

Jeri L. Stortz, SW
CFSM, Inc.

Enclosures

Letter to Shannon Gibney regarding "non-identifying information."

**Child and Family
Services of Michigan, Inc.**

The Family . . .
our concern for
over 100 years.

2157 University Park Drive
Post Office Box 348
Okemos, Michigan
48805

517/349-6226

**Member:
Local United Ways**

Member of:
Child Welfare
League of America

Family Service America

Michigan Association
of Children's Alliances

Michigan Federation of Private
Child and Family Agencies

Accredited by:*
Council on Accreditation
of Services for Families
and Children, Inc.

Member Agency
Locations:

Adrian*

Alpena

Battle Creek*

Holland*

Holt*

Howell

Jackson*

Kalamazoo*

Midland*

St. Joseph

Traverse City

October 10, 1994

Ms. Shannon Elaine Gibney

Dear Ms. Gibney:

In response to your request for identifying information, we have checked the Central Registry and there were no consents on file. However, there was an inquiry in the record and our agency has had contact with your birth mother. She has recently signed her consent authorizing our agency to release her name and location to you.

Your birth mother is:

Patricia Ellen Powers born, 11/14/55

Phone:

Your name at birth was: Erin Rebecca Powers

Some people find it helpful to talk about their thoughts and feelings as they are making decisions about re-connecting with their biological relatives. If it would be helpful to you to discuss any issues you may have regarding your birth, adoption, or the above information, please contact me at the above address.

Sincerely,

Jeri L. Stortz, SW
Post Adoption Worker

Enclosures   1-800-

Follow-up letter to Shannon Gibney regarding "non-identifying information."

You were born, 01/30/75 at St. Joseph Mercy Hospital in Ann Arbor, Michigan. At birth you weighed 5 lbs. and 15 oz. and you were 19" in length. You arrived 6:12 a.m. and you had black hair, blue eyes and average build. You were described as very alert and responsive. There were no known abnormalities or birth injuries noted. You were placed in a foster home until you joined your adoptive family on 06/10/75.

The status of termination was voluntary. Your birth mother felt that adoptive planning would serve in your best interest. She was unmarried and felt unable to emotionally and financially provide for you.

Your adoption was finalized, 09/17/76 through the Ingham County Probate Court.

Your birthmother was 19 at the time of your birth. She had brown hair, brown eyes and a fair complexion. She stood 5'3" and weighed 105 lbs. She was a high school graduate and was employed as a waitress. She was of Irish descent and followed the Catholic faith. She was described as in good health. Your birthmother was described as above average intelligence. She had three brothers, ages 15, 14 and 13 and three sisters, ages 26, 25, and 9.

Your maternal grandmother was 51 at the time of your birth. She had brown hair, brown eyes and a fair complexion. She stood 5' and was described as plump. She had attended college and was employed as a secretary. She was of Irish descent and followed the Catholic faith. She had mild diabetes.

Your maternal grandfather was 51 at the time of your birth. He had gray hair, blue eyes and a fair complexion. He stood 5'5" and was described as small and thin. He had completed the two years of college and was employed as an accountant. He was of Irish descent and followed the Catholic faith. He was described as alcoholic with a history of heart trouble.

Your birthfather was of Afro-American descent and was employed as a musician. He played the guitar in a band. He was discharged from the U.S. Air Force for psychiatric reasons. His educational level, religious affiliation, age, height or weight was not stated.

There was no additional information regarding the paternal side of your family.

Boise Collins – Air Force.
Grandparents lived in Detroit. They wanted custody.

You were born, 1/30/75 at St. Joseph Mercy Hospital in Ann Arbor, Michigan. At birth you weighed 5 lbs. and 15 oz. and you were 19" in length. You arrived 6:12 a.m. and you had black hair, blue eyes and average build. You were described as very alert and responsive. There were no known abnormalities or birth injuries noted. You were placed in a foster home until you joined your adoptive family on 6/10/75.

The status of termination was voluntary. Your birth mother felt that adoptive planning would serve in your best interest. She was unmarried and felt unable to emotionally and financially provide for you.

Your birthmother was 19 at the time of your birth. She had brown hair, brown eyes and a fair complexion. She stood 5'3" and weighed 105 lbs. She was a high school graduate and was employed as a waitress. She was of Irish descent and followed the Catholic faith. She was described as in good health. Your birthmother was described as above average intelligence. She had three brothers, ages 15, 14 and 13 and three sisters, ages 26, 25, and 9.

Your maternal grandmother was 51 at the time of your birth. She had brown hair, brown eyes and a fair complexion. She stood 5' and was described as plump. She had attended college and was employed as a secretary. She was of Irish descent and followed the Catholic faith. She had mild diabetes.

Your maternal grandfather was 51 at the time of your birth. He had gray hair, blue eyes and a fair complexion. He stood 5'5" and was described as small and thin. He had completed two years of college and was employed as an accountant. He was of Irish descent and followed the Catholic faith. He was described as an alcoholic with a history of heart trouble.

Your birthfather was of Afro-American descent and was employed as a musician. He played the guitar in a band. He was discharged from the U.S. Air Force for psychiatric reasons. His educational level, religious affiliation, age, height or weight was not stated.

There was no additional information regarding the paternal side of your family.

From a Mother's Day Card Patricia sent to Susan Gibney.

. . . *Since 1975 I too had many hopes, wishes, wonderings, imaginings, etc., etc., re: Shannon (who I still know as Erin), and you. It wasn't until the laws in Michigan changed and I was given the opportunity to put my name and some of my family members names into the "National Registry." That opened the door for Shannon to find me or my family members in case I was dead. As we both have seen, Shannon is not too thrilled with me at this time. It is unfortunate. I have a close friend who was adopted. She met her birth mother when she was in her late 30s and accepted her and never once criticized or judged her. I am certain though that I too possess some of the same traits Shannon does. Thankfully, life experience and time has mellowed me. So, Sue, you and Jim can rest assured that some of these challenging traits are genetic. As Shannon has brought her spark of life into your hearts, I believe most assuredly that you and Jim have provided her with a solid foundation of unconditional love that her restless spirit will always call home and Mother . . .*

Dear Sue,

Thank you so much for that beautiful card, pin, and most especially, for your kind, compassionate words. It all touched my heart and moved me to tears -- that's a good thing!

Since 1975 I too had many hopes, wishes, wonderings, imaginings, etc., etc., re: Shannon (who I still knew as Erin), and you. It wasn't until the laws in Michigan changed and I was given the opportunity to "put my name and some of my family members names into the "National Registry," that opened the door for Shannon to find me or my family members in case I was dead. As we both have seen, Shannon is not too thrilled with me at this time. It is unfortunate. I have a close friend who was adopted. She met her birth mother when she was in her late 30's and accepted her and never once criticized or judged her. I am certain though that I too possess some of the same traits that Shannon does. And time has mellowed me. So, Sue, you and Jim thank fully, life experience and time has mellowed me. So, Sue, you and Jim can rest assured that some of these challenging traits are genetic. As Shannon can rest assured that some of these challenging traits are genetic. I believe most assuredly that you and Jim have provided her with a solid foundation of unconditional

-2-
love that her restless spirit will always call home and Mother. I thank you.

From the moment we met, I felt connected to your spirit. I know you are a spiritual, life-giving force for good in this difficult world; the essence of "Mother." I am blessed that Shannon has you and Jim, and John and Ben. I must admit, I was a little (Tender Thoughts) afraid of Jim when I first met him. Please -- no disrespect intended -- I think it's just the engineer thing' -- and truth be told, none of you knew at that time what a harmless creature I am. As I said on the phone, I couldn't have wished for a better family for that wonderful creature we knew and love as Shannon.

Please accept this pin Sue. I teach 7-8th grade religious ed. in Utica's inner city. I think this is a witness (the church thing).

Tender Thoughts Greetings
1460 The Queensway
Toronto, Ontario M8Z 1S7
© AGC, Inc.
MADE IN U.S.A.

305TTM 43445-04P

61520 55078
3677390

It doesn't take
a day like this
To think of you, but still—
Special days bring special thoughts
And Mother's Day always will.

Have a Happy Day

With Thoughts of You
ON MOTHER'S DAY

UTICA, NEW YORK. JANUARY 30, 1977

AND JANUARY 30, 1978

AND JANUARY 30, 1979

AND JANUARY 30, 1980

AND JANUARY 30, 1981

AND JANUARY 30, 1982

AND JANUARY 30, 1983

AND JANUARY 30, 1984

AND JANUARY 30, 1985

"Etc. etc."

SHE STANDS ON THE SIDE OF THE HIGHWAY, thumb out.

She is still wearing last night's T-shirt from her shift at the bar, and her old jeans, ripped in the knees. Her huge Utica College sweatshirt is tied loosely around her waist, and she has "borrowed" her sister Kathleen's down jacket for the trip. A small knapsack is slung over her right shoulder, containing all her worldly possessions: three pairs of underwear, her other pair of jeans, a bra, a pair of socks, and a pocketknife. Of course, she snuck a bottle of Captain Morgan rum and a pack of cigarettes in there as well. It's a long way to Ann Arbor, and she doesn't want to be caught somewhere strange without a sip or a drag. Rum has a way of warming you from the inside out, and it could very well be a cold, wet trip. She thumbs the wad of bills in her pocket. In total, she has fifty-five dollars and forty-six cents, the sum of her last paycheck. She won't be coming back to work at the bar any time soon, though, not after the brawl last night. She blacked out after the first punch, although her bruised jaw remembers there was more.

A black Trans Am with a gold-and-brown Firebird plastered across its hood whizzes past, and a white teenager leans out the shotgun window to yell, "Nice ass!" She can see his friend, the driver, laughing appreciatively beside him.

"Dicks," she says under her breath. Why are men so disgusting? She can spot someone who is drowning their sorrows in a bottle a mile away when she is bartending, and it softens her wary protective shell, despite her knowing better. But then the man will misinterpret kindness for sexual interest, he will say something untoward, and she will lose her cool and end up shouting or worse. Rudy has fired and then rehired her three times already because of this.

The misguided Trans Am honks down Route 8 until it is a small black dot on the horizon. Then the landscape swallows it up. She silently prays they will crash. Then she chastises herself for having such a horrible thought.

There is just a little bit of wind today, but on the whole, the weather is fair for January in Utica. Snow, now brown from the dirt on the road and exhaust from the cars, piles up in drifts beside her. And it is twenty-two degrees, so much warmer than it could be. Still, she should have grabbed Kathleen's gloves as well as her jacket. She cups her pale, ashy hands for a moment, coughs, then blows air into them. The skin is red and chapped. Then she turns her palms toward her and studies the patchwork of lines there. The long ones across the top, and the shorter one that curves down toward her wrist. Someone told her once that that means she will have a short life. It wouldn't surprise her. She has always felt that her life ended the moment that Erin was taken from her, anyway. The best part of her life, anyway.

Someone waves at her from inside of a pale pink Mustang speeding by, and before she has time to react, a gray Firebird and a dirty brown minivan follow closely behind it, honking. People having way too much fun on the road for their own—or anyone else's—good.

Finally, a semi with a picture of a giant robot that transforms into a jet from panel to panel, and the words "Macross Saga Fighters: Collect Them All!" splashed across its side, slows down and starts to pull off the highway. She sees the driver waving to her, inside the cab. She tightens her grip on the handles of her knapsack. *Maybe this time, I'll go.* She waves back.

The eighteen-wheeler pulls up a few feet behind her, its brakes exhaling loudly. She walks up to the passenger door, and the driver leans over and opens it.

"Mornin'!" he says pleasantly. He is a balding middle-aged white man with a belly that spills over the top of his pants. His eyes are kind, though, and despite the overpowering stench emanating from the Smurfette air freshener dangling from his CB, she thinks he won't try anything.

"Where you headed?" he asks easily.

"Through Canada," she says. "But I'll get on for however far you're going."

He laughs, and his belly rumbles. "Well, I ain't headed that far, I can tell ya. Will Rochester do ya?"

She smiles; Rochester is almost a third of the way! "That would really help me out," she says.

"Well, come on up then, gal, and let's get going already!" He laughs again, and she is surprised to learn that it is a pleasant sound in her ears. It reminds her of her father's laughter when she was young, before he started drinking: unabashed and infectious. The driver motions for her to step up.

She does, and as soon as she sits down, a bright yellow Camaro, a bit rusty on the top, pulls off the highway and then right in front of them. Patricia sighs.

The semi driver looks at her in confusion. "You know them?"

Patricia shakes her head as Rich begins laying on the horn. "Yes, I know them," she says quietly.

She hears two car doors slam, and then the sound of feet crunching gravel and snow. Then Bridget's red wool hat is at the door, and her sister's dark brown eyes are looking up at her sadly.

When she pulls open the door, the driver throws a fat arm around Patricia protectively. "Whoa now," he says to Bridget. "We don't want no trouble here."

Bridget laughs. "Well, then, you sure don't want to give my sister a ride."

Patricia clutches her knapsack tighter. "You're not supposed to be here, Bridget." She turns her head away from her, and refocuses on the highway, and the dozens of cars racing past. *This time, I'm going.*

"No, *you're* not supposed to be here, Pat," says Bridget. There is an edge in her voice. She doesn't want to reach for her big sister because she knows how easily she gets spooked.

"Now, what's going on here, little lady?" the driver says to Patricia. "Is this really your sister?"

Patricia eyes him warily. Then she nods.

He slowly moves his arm away from her. "You want to get out, then, and go with them?" he asks.

Rich, who Patricia calls Bridget's "budget boyfriend," leans into Bridget, his exercise clothing wet with sweat. Patricia rolls her eyes; Bridget must have grabbed him straight from a workout and told him it was "an emergency" again.

"Now, you need to come with us, Pat," Rich tells her. "This has gone far enough."

Patricia feels her pulse quicken, her blood screaming in her ears. "Fuck off, Rich," she says before she can think.

Rich's face becomes bloated with anger, and he lunges for her.

Patricia scoots away from him, toward the driver, who allows her to smush into him. It's the closest he's been to a woman in over a year. "Whoa, son!" the driver yells to Rich. "You need to back off."

Rich's hand grazes the edge of Patricia's coat, but it slides off the slippery nylon. Bridget pulls him back, and the two of them talk in hushed tones to the side. Rich is a full-time bodybuilder who fixes cars when he's not buying new vitamin supplements. Bridget has been dating him for a year now, and no one in the family can stand him.

"You're really gonna let that crazy bitch sister of yours talk to me like that? That's really okay with you, now?"

"No, of course it's not okay with me! But we need to get her out of here and back home safe, and then we can deal with that. One thing at a time," she says, rubbing his arm.

"Meathead," Patricia says under her breath.

The driver looks from Patricia to Rich and Bridget, back to Patricia again. "You sure got an interesting family, little lady," he says.

Patricia snorts and scoots herself a few inches away from him. "You have no idea."

Bridget maneuvers herself so she is in front of Rich. She looks straight into Patricia's eyes, pleadingly. "Look, I know this is a rough day," she says. "I mean, I know it is the worst day of the year for you. Every year."

Patricia feels tears sting the edges of her eyes, and looks away. "You don't know shit," she says, but her voice is breaking.

Bridget takes a deep breath. "I know you may think that . . . but I lost a child, too, you know."

Her head whips back at her sister, fury lacing every movement. "It's not the same thing! Miscarriage is not the same . . ." And then the tears come, precisely because she doesn't want them to. Precisely because she is doing everything she can to hold them back.

Bridget lays her hand over her big sister's. "I know it's not the same. And I know I can never really know what it's like for you." Her voice gets soft.

Patricia puts her hand over her mouth, because the tears are turning into sobs. *"She'd be two today. She'd be five. Six. Seven. Eight. What are her adoptive parents doing for her birthday? What does she like? Is she into Strawberry Shortcake, or is she a tomboy like I was, and would rather just climb a tree? What kind of cake does she like? Does she ever think of me, wonder about me? Does she feel as lost as I do without her?"* She can feel the cool glass of the bottle of rum through the knapsack, and she wants to open it and take a long, full swig. She wants to tell her sister that it hurts more than she will ever know, that it's like someone cut off a limb and is now walking around with it acting like it's theirs, but that her bleeding body remembers. That the wound will never heal, will never close up.

"I'm going to get her," she whispers through the tears.

Everyone and everything has grown eerily quiet: Rich, the driver, Bridget. Like they are at a funeral or wake, watching someone completely fall apart while paying their respects to a beloved. There is a deflated quality to the air now—all the sparks and anger have dissipated. Patricia herself feels suddenly exhausted, and wants nothing more than to crawl into her bed under her covers. For a lifetime.

Bridget steps up into the cab, and sits next to her sister. She puts her arm around her and pulls her into her chest. "You can't," she whispers back. "You don't even know where she is."

"I do," Patricia whimpers into her sweater. "Yes, I do."

Bridget sighs. "But you don't know where in Ann Arbor she is."

Patricia pulls back and sits up. She dries her eyes. "I'll find her. I know I can."

Bridget shakes her head. "Pat . . . it's against the law."

Patricia wipes her nose with the back of her hand. "The law's what took her from me in the first place."

Bridget squeezes her hand tightly. "I know, but . . . Besides all that, you gave her up for a reason, didn't you? I love you, you're my sister and you're a good person, but . . . Even through all this, isn't she better off?"

Patricia doesn't want to hear this. It is the truth she lives with for three hundred and sixty-four days a year. Just let her live with this other truth, her truth, this one day a year. The truth of a mother's love for her daughter. The truth of a love that never ends, no matter the lifetime, timeline, family line, relinquishment, or adoption. She weeps louder now, and the sobs rack the whole cab. They are sobs that she has been saving up the whole year, so they are sobs that could break open atoms, rip the very fabric of space-time.

The men look away in embarrassment. The driver needs to get back on the road, and says as much.

Bridget nods, and helps her sister out of the cab, and back onto the cold, solid road. She walks with her carefully to the Camaro, and lays her down in the back seat. She puts a rough, thick blanket over her for the short ride to the apartment. She knew to bring it, from last year.

Shannon Gibney/Erin Powers, 1978.

PART TWO

Infinite selves, recursive pathways

"STABILITY AND SECURITY" are words you hear birth mothers say frequently in relationship to their relinquished children. As in, "She needed stability and security, and that was something I couldn't give her. So, I decided it would be better for her to be raised by people who could."

Most biological parents of adoptees are young, lower-income, and have little education beyond high school at the time of relinquishment. The relationship that produced the child, if it is a relationship at all, is not what many would describe as long-term. In contrast, most adoptive parents are older, upper middle class or even rich, married, and have college degrees.

Housing.

Food and clothing.

Education.

Middle-class values.

These are the things that produce "stability and security" in parents and families—which they can then transfer to their children—according to the vast majority of child psychologists, child welfare experts, policymakers, and the general public.

A solid understanding of racism and Black racial identity do not produce "stability and security" for a Black child in this formulation.

Nor does a real connection to local Black communities.

Knowledge of an origin story or family health history are also seen as ancillary to a child's stability and security in the way that adoption has been practiced historically—and in how it is still practiced today.

It is true that poverty can definitely make a child's home life unstable. And as an adoptee, I do believe that most birth mothers are making the best decisions they can given the information, options, and frameworks presented to them. But why are these the dominant frameworks presented to them—and all of us? And how are stability and security actually experienced in the lives of children? As unambiguously positive forces? We have all been children, so we all know it is not simply a matter of education and economics.

DECEMBER 2008.

Patricia Powers to Susan Gibney.

. . . I am happy to hear that Shannon is doing so well. I do not hold out hope that she will ever understand how much I love and care for her, and how grateful I am that you and your husband Jim are who you are. You gave her the chance for a secure, happy life. A life I was completely unable to give her back then. I will always keep you, your husband, of course Shannon, and your family (the boys)—in my heart, and in my prayers. I do wish things could be different. But being as they are I am eternally grateful. You are everything I wanted in a mother for Shannon. Thank you.

Love,

Patricia

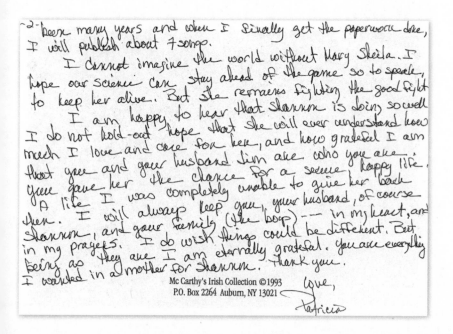

-2- been many years and when I finally get the paperwork done, I will publish about 7 songs.

I cannot imagine the world without Mary Sheila. I hope our science can stay ahead of the game so to speak, to keep her alive. But she remains fighting the good fight

I am happy to hear that Shannon is doing so well I do not hold-out hope that she will ever understand how much I love and care for her, and how grateful I am that you and your husband Jim are who you are. You gave her the chance for a secure, happy life. A life I was completely unable to give her back then. I will always keep you, your husband, of course Shannon, and your family (the boys) — in my heart, and in my prayers. I do wish things could be different. But being as they are I am eternally grateful. You are everything I wanted in a mother for Shannon. Thank you.

McCarthy's Irish Collection ©1993
P.O. Box 2264 Auburn, NY 13021

Love,
Patricia

From a story by Shannon Gibney, age seven.

1.

Once there lived a Girl named Shella She lived in an orfenige with some other Girls. Ofen she looked out of window at the ███ ▪ neighbors horse named Goldey But Shella wanted to call him Paleiwam. But she never was allowed to go over and see him because the lady that took care of the horse didnt allow little girls like Shella to get hurt. But Shella new that Paleiwam ███ wouldn't hurt eneyone. and She wanted to prove It! But how? Shella decided to ███ ride Paleiwam the next night.

6.

IN The MORNG she gave paliewam a breakfast of break and butter with some water after all she had plentey. She had a piece of bread some milk. after that Shella decided to billed a hut. she worked and wocked and worked. unil it was done at nihit she stoped aND she looked at it. it was done in the monings she would make Paleiwam a stable. Paleiwam was Hungrey so she gave him a peice of bread and water and she had a cookie and they went to sleep a week past. they went back to the house. someone had come to bay a offen orfen. they bought Shella. they let her take paliewam to!

The END!

From the first and last pages of a short story by seven-year-old Shannon about an orphan girl who steals a horse.

Shannon Gibney is eight.

"BUT HOW DO YOU KNOW THAT I'M NOT A ROBOT?" the girl asks her mother. They are seated on rickety folding chairs in the backyard, the long shadow of the treehouse behind them.

The girl's mother sighs. "Because you have skin, and bones, and blood," she says. "Plus, you're breathing."

The girl frowns. "But they could have robots that could do that."

The girl's mother peers at her. "Do what?"

"Breathe. Like in *The Six Million Dollar Man*," says the girl. She and her two brothers watch the show with their father religiously.

"Shannon . . ." The girl's mother trails off. This is not the first conversation like this she has had with her daughter, who she has told on many occasions has an "overactive imagination."

"Mom, I'm serious!" the girl exclaims, with the vehemence of an eight-year-old. "I could be a new prototype. Designed by someone in an alternate universe. Another timeline or something. Another dimension. And I could have a chip in my brain making me say and do everything I say and do. Making me think—and you, and Dad, and Jon, and Ben—that I am the *real* Shannon Gibney. When all along I am really just *a fake*. And you would never know it." The girl frowns, then shifts in her seat uncomfortably. Now she is getting to what is *really* bothering her. "*I* would never know it." A flutter of something—anxiety is what she will learn to call it later—flips in her stomach.

"Honey," her mother says, taking her hand. Her daughter is her most difficult child, but for some reason, this makes her love her more. "You know that you're here now, with me."

Shannon is looking off into the distance, at the woods behind their house. She and her brothers and friends and cousins play back there frequently, building forts, and digging holes, and becoming kings and queens and dragons. It is a place of magic and mystery. It is a place right beside home, but far enough away from it to be someplace else entirely. It is somewhere to go when you cannot really go anywhere. And there is a light inside it right now, faint, but growing under a low tree branch.

The girl's mother reaches over to her and takes her chin in her hand, directing her eyes to her own. "Right?" she asks.

Shannon nods, distracted. "Yes," she says. "We're here. Now."

"So we know at least that much is true, right?" her mother asks.

The girl works to focus on her mother and her words, but it is hard, with the light in the woods on the periphery of her sights. "I guess."

Her mother lets go of her chin. "That's all we can know, sometimes. What's here and now. What could be, what could have been, what will be . . ."

Shannon sees the light contracting in the woods, and she grips the faded wood of her folding chair. "What's happening now, somewhere else . . . ," she says.

"All of that is just . . ." Her mom waves her hands. "Possibility."

The girl forces herself to pay attention to her mother, although what she wants more than anything is to run to the woods and seek out the light. To see where it's coming from, and perhaps discern its meaning. "Possibilities," she says, correcting her mother.

"Yes," her mother says. "Possibilities. We can never know without a doubt that you *aren't* an amazing bionic robot, and that there aren't multiple dimensions happening simultaneously, as you say . . ."

The light is now gone, has diminished completely. But the girl has

the sense that it will be back again, and soon. And that there is something there for her, in those woods. "Or that there aren't multiple *me*'s
living out their lives right now, on different timelines," she says.

Her mother, whose blond hair is pulled back in a clip at the nape of
her neck, squeezes her daughter's hand harder. Her only daughter, whom
they adopted at five months because they wanted a daughter more than
anything, and here she is. Here she is, the quirky, funny, smart, oddball
little mixed Black girl in their family. "That could certainly be true," her
mother says slowly. "It all depends on what you believe. And the little
that we know, as human beings. And since we know that we're here
now together, why worry about those infinite other possibilities? I know
you're not a robot, my dear." Her mother laughs. "I'm sorry, I know you
want to believe you're special . . . and you are . . . but not like that."

The girl laughs, too. She can't help it. Even she has to admit that her
mind gets the best of her sometimes. She shakes her head. "No, I don't
want to be a robot!"

Her mother yanks playfully on one of her braids. "Good. Because I
don't want to raise a robot." She stands up. "Come on. Let's go in and
see if your brothers want a Popsicle."

I stand up, too, then and hug my mom. She always makes me feel
like things are okay, like I am maybe not as crazy as my mind can make
me feel sometimes.

The girl jumps up and down, and yells, "Popsicles!" hoping that her
brothers will hear her in the den.

Something flashes from the woods, and she stops, startled.

"What?" Mom asks, her hand resting carefully on my shoulder.

Shannon peers at the woods, and the woods peers back. *There's
something there,* a faint gravelly man's voice says in her ear. She doesn't
recognize it, and shakes her head. "Nothing," she says, turning away.

There is no light in the woods. It is gone.

"Let's go in."

Shannon Gibney is ten.

THE BUS PULLS UP at the corner of Brandywine and Terhune at eight fifteen a.m., packed full of screaming, laughing children with full backpacks and carefully combed hair. Jon, Shannon, and Ben line up dutifully behind the six other kids at the bus stop, most of them not really awake, bumping into each other to get on first. We always line up toward the back of the line, because we don't really care which seats we take, and we also don't care to get into fights with stupid kids. Mostly, we just try to keep ourselves out of situations that could be troublesome. Blending in is always best in the Gibney paradigm, although I always seem to have the most trouble doing that. For various reasons.

I slowly move down the bus aisle, surveying open seats. We are one of the last stops, so there is really only one open, but it is next to Sherice, who wears Jordache and Guess jeans, who has colorful beads in her long braids, who pops her gum, and is always cracking jokes I don't get in class. I would rather sit next to Tom, who has short blond hair, is obsessed with rockets and football, and who for some reason has a crush on me.

"Hey, Shannon," he says as I slide in beside him.

I wince inside. I do not want him to like me. It makes my skin itch. "Hi," I say.

"Did you watch *Robotech*? The whole protoculture revelation? That blew my mind."

She smiles, in spite of herself. Tom watches *Robotech* as religiously as she and her brothers do, and always has a book he's reading, which is why he uses words like *revelation*.

"Yeah, it was cool," she says. "Real cool how they seeded the universe, even Earth. But those Zentraedi . . . They are *tricky*. Rick and them were right to come at them with everything they got."

Tom nods, and the bus roars back to life. Then they are suddenly jerking forward, headed toward Pattengill Elementary School. It is on the other side of town, so it will take a minute to get there. It is called an "open" public school and is an experiment in progressive pedagogy. Kids do not sit in rows and listen to boring math lessons, like they did at their other school. They do not all read the same book that no one really likes and then sit around and talk about *the main idea*. At the start of each week, the girl sits down with her teacher and decides what her goals are in reading and math, and then they map out how she will get there. Working with other students is encouraged, and no one accuses you of cheating if you do. She gets to pick out the books she wants to read, like *The Phantom Tollbooth*, *Anastasia Krupnik*, *Lassie Come-Home*, and *Superfudge*. Shannon loves all of it. She leaps out of bed in the morning and can't wait to get to school. "They just weren't challenging her enough at Pittsfield," her mom told Mrs. Sperling at their last conference. "I think she was just bored and checked out most of the time. This school is a godsend for us."

The girl is so engaged in breaking down the *Robotech* saga with Tom that the fifteen-minute bus ride flies by, and she forgets that she is on the bus at all until they pull up to the front of the school, and the driver opens the doors.

The girl is feeding Pez, the classroom chinchilla, right before recess. She has been instructed not to open the small door too wide, as Pez is both fast and intelligent, and has managed to escape on many occasions. He stands as if at attention, nibbling each pellet with his formidable front teeth. She smiles at him, hoping he is enjoying his meal as much as she enjoys the BLTs her dad makes her on weekends. Someone taps her on the shoulder, but the girl pretends not to notice. She knows who it is.

"Shannon!" Gillian Price hisses in her ear. She is the most popular girl in class, partly due to her looks and partly due to her vicious social tactics.

I roll my eyes and pet Pez as he chews. I have never liked girls like Gillian, with their perfectly white skin, and perfectly blue eyes, and perfectly symmetrical features to match their desperate ambitions for popularity.

Gillian turns me around. "Freddie told Sarah who told me that Tom likes you!" She shuffles her new Tretorns on the latex floor, and studies me carefully. "Barf me out, right?"

I look at my worn-down loafers My skin is itching again, and I don't want Gillian to see it. I wouldn't give her the satisfaction. I like Tom. Tom is *nice*, but I don't *like* like him. I turn back to the chinchilla's cage and shut the door.

But Gillian, of course, will not be ignored.

"What are you going to do?" she asks, all up in my face.

I can see the red of a pimple growing just beneath the otherwise dull mask of her forehead. On the other side of the room, I see Tom writing something carefully, deliberately, on lined paper. I think he is working on the book he is making about the *Challenger*. He is not a bad artist, and has showed me very detailed pictures of engines and other devices I didn't even know were there.

"I mean, what if he asks you out?" Gillian's blue eyes are suddenly huge and look like they might burst from excitement. I realize that she and Ellen and Kristy, her friends with mouths just as big as hers, have been talking over these possibilities for some time. I reach my right hand over to my left forearm and start to scratch it. Hard. It reddens and the skin begins to flake, but I keep scratching. The itch keeps growing.

"I gotta get back to my book," the girl tells Gillian. She is writing and illustrating the second in a series of mystery stories for kids about Tia, Tim, and Jim, a sibling sleuth team. Halfway to her desk, she realizes that it is across from Tom's. Which wasn't a problem when they walked into class this morning, deep in discussions about *The Macross Saga* and the inevitability of a Zentraedi annihilation, but which is now very much A Problem.

When Shannon reaches her desk, she slumps down in her seat miserably. Dramatically. Why can't she just be Rick Hunter, star fighter pilot, defeating invading enemy combatants at every turn, when there is no hope left? Why can't she spend her time mastering Robotechnology, and learning the secrets of protoculture?

Tom eyes her cautiously, a red pencil in his hand. "Hey," he says.

"Hey," she replies back. She eyes his worn Ocean Pacific T-shirt, and his acid-washed jeans. He would make a decent partner to ambush the Zentraedi with. Too bad there are none around here, just the likes of Gillian and co.

"Working on the mystery book?" He angles his colored pencil a bit, shading the blast of an aft rocket.

"Yeah, about to," she says. She opens up her desk, and lifts out the loose pages and cardboard covers bundled together with a rubber band.

"Cool," he says. "Can't wait to read it."

She feels her face color, and the itch on her forearm swell with a vengeance. She wishes he weren't so nice to her. She wishes they could just go back to the beginning of the year, when she was just another kid in line at recess or at lunch, not the object of his affections. He probably won't even try to get her out at dodgeball anymore. It's all bogus.

She arranges everything on her desk carefully: the papers with a few chapters scratched onto them, the papers with nothing scratched onto them yet, the cardboard cover and back, and the new box of crayons her grandmother gave her last week, especially for illustrating the book.

They knew they were not alone, she writes at the beginning of Chapter 3. *Just like kids always know when they are not alone. They just didn't know what to do about it, or where the mystery started or ended. In fact, they didn't even know what the mystery was at this point. But Tia had an idea, and like always, her brothers had to follow it.*

Then it is like all there is the story, and the questions that make the story go on, and the characters stuck in it try to find their way, like a web. Gradually, the girl feels her shoulders relax, her skin breathe. She is in the classroom writing across from Tom, but she is also in the basement of the haunted mansion, guiding the three siblings to safety through the twisted staircase to the first floor. After she writes the part where Tim and Jim get captured by the Red Hawk, she puts down her pencil and stretches. She looks across the desk, but Tom isn't there. Funny, she hadn't even seen him leave. He must have gone to the bathroom. She looks up at the daily schedule on the board: recess at 10:50. That's in two minutes. That means a kickball game in three minutes. She is glad she ignored her mother's suggestion to wear her tennis shoes today, instead of her loafers. They are worn and stained, but she likes them that way because she can play kickball in them so much better. When they were new last year, her feet were smaller and always slipping around their too-big insides, and when she kicked the ball, her shoe would always go flying. Now, though, the hand-me-down, synthetic leather shoes pinch her toes. They are like second skin, sticking to her feet exactly, stopping and going exactly when she needs them to.

Shannon's gaze shifts from her loafers to something bright beside them on the floor. She leans down, curious, and picks up the small round object. It is a tack, she discovers. Someone has dropped it on the floor. She should give it to Mrs. Sperling; that is what she should do. That way, no one will step or slip on it and get hurt. That is exactly what she will do. And that is what she does. She stands up and walks over to Mrs. Sperling's wide oak desk. It is littered with paper and also a coffee mug out of which Mrs. Sperling is always drinking tea. Mrs. Sperling is not at her desk. She is on the other side of the room, helping Nikky with his work plan for the week. Shannon takes the tack and slowly brings it toward a small plastic blue cup, which contains rubber bands, eraser tips for pencils, paper clips, and other paraphernalia. Shannon knows she should put the tack in the catchall container, can actually *see* herself doing it. But somehow, her hand doesn't quite make it there. The tack remains in her palm, and she finds herself walking slowly to Tom's chair, looking back and forth, from the tack to the chair. Then she watches her right hand take the tack from her palm, and slowly, deliberately, place it faceup on the seat. I walk away very quickly, all the way out of the classroom and into the hallway, where Gillian and her friends are huddled around a table, working on a math problem.

"Hey, Shannon," Ellen says amicably. She is the nicest of the three of them. We might even be friends if the other two weren't constantly around.

"Hey," I say, looking around nervously.

"Did you solve this problem? We think we got it, but we're not sure." She gestures toward their paper, and I reluctantly come closer. It is an advanced problem, with a bunch of six-digit numbers. I stare at it hard, until the digits start bleeding into each other. Then I blink.

"No, I'm almost there," I say, which is a lie. I am about three pages behind all the other advanced math students. And I am also engaged in a long con with Mrs. Sperling about my progress in learning my times tables: She thinks I know them all, when really I know almost none of them. And would like to keep it that way.

Suddenly, a shriek erupts from the classroom. It is loud and long and sharp. Definitely male.

I dive under the table.

"Wha—?" says Gillian.

"Don't ask," I say.

Gillian sticks her now red-faced head down to my level, and says, "What did you do?"

The shriek has now changed to a low moan, and I can hear Mrs. Sperling using her soothing tone, so it must be pretty bad. I imagine Tom's butt permanently stuck with a tack, and I want to laugh. I imagine Tom with tears running down his cheeks because of the pain, and a well of regret bursts in me. "I put a tack on Tom's seat."

Ellen and Kristy have now stuck their heads down to where Gillian and I are under the table, and their mouths form surprised little Os.

"That's bad," Kristy says quietly.

My stomach knots. I try to fold myself into a smaller ball.

"He has a crush on her," Ellen tells them.

"No duh, but that's no reason to put a tack on his chair," Gillian fires back. "You can really hurt somebody that way."

Mrs. Sperling walks out of the classroom, her arm around Tom. Tom's face is shielded from me. He's staring at the floor, so I can't see if he's crying. I wish I could take it back.

"Is Shannon out here?" Mrs. Sperling asks Gillian, Ellen, and Kristy.

They stumble over themselves to get in their seats, then nod and point under the table.

I dust myself off and emerge from the floor. Mrs. Sperling used to put her arm around me when she tutored me in math last year.

"Please come to the office with us," she says evenly. Of course Mrs. Sperling knows it was me. She knows me inside and out.

Tom still won't look at me. His gaze seems to be locked on a brick in the wall beside us. But he isn't crying, although he looks very sad.

I nod and follow behind them. When we get to the office, I admit what I have done and apologize. And then I am the one who is crying.

The girl grabs a long and brittle branch lying on the forest floor. It is almost the right size for the wall of the fort she is building. Almost. When she places it with the rest of the branches she has stacked up against the blackgum tree, it falls. She harrumphs, and picks it up again, attempting to put it in exactly the same place. It falls again.

"Argh!"

Her little brother, digging a hole beside her, stops momentarily to ask her what's wrong.

This makes her madder, for some reason.

"It. Won't. Stay. Up!" she says. This time, however, she tries to lodge the bottom of the branch into the soil, thinking that it just might need a solid base to remain upright. But the skinny wood just collapses, and the girl kicks at the dirt in frustration.

"Shan!" Ben yells at me. "You're messing it all up."

At Jon's instruction, we kids are creating a kingdom for a new species of giant ants. Our older brother is very smart and insists that he has discovered some back here in our enchanted forest. Jon has told us that these new, fantastic giant ants will need small stick houses to live in, with small ant beds inside to lay on. And even an ant bathroom outside of each dwelling, which Ben is in charge of.

"Whatever," the girl mumbles. "It's already all messed up anyway. Look." She grabs the errant branch and throws it toward the rest of the towering trees that create a kind of cave around them. When they are back here, it is like they are in a completely different place, a secret hideaway only visible to kids. The air even smells different here—musty and old and even wet sometimes. I often wonder if it is the air from another era, from olden times, that somehow got trapped underneath all the leaves and dirt and scrub, so that when we breathe, we are also transported to that other olden time. Lying on my stomach, I peer back at the house, breathing in the dirt and rousting around in the sticks and leaves and bugs and debris. The house looks almost like it is from a distant future, some imagined place that doesn't even exist yet. The sliding glass door and the shuttered windows of our modest home look strange to my suddenly feral eyes, and only become familiar to me again once I am back on our safe, green lawn.

"It's not messed up," Ben insists. "You just have to know how to do it." He stands, not bothering to dust off the dirt that now covers him head to toe, and gently places the stick beside the others on the emerging fort wall. It stays up.

The girl sighs and shakes her head. Then she throws her arm around her little brother. "How do you always do that?"

He grins his nine-year-old grin. "Magic!" They both laugh. When something doesn't work, Ben is the person to ask. Mostly because he has reserves of patience, while the girl seems to have been born without any.

The girl begins thrashing around in the scrub beside them. "We need more branches," she says.

Her brother grunts his agreement beside her, already back at work thrusting a stick into a rapidly growing hole.

And it is then that she sees it: a small circle with a spiral center, moving on the forest floor. It is bright, sending out mostly white light, but occasionally you can see specks of violet and blue and even green flying out of it. "Ben!" she yells.

"I'll fix it in a minute," he says absently, never taking his eyes off of his stick and the ground.

I jump back from the whirling funnel about a foot in front of me, and then hit Ben lightly on his head. "No, look!"

He waves me off absently, but finally looks up. Shock spreads across his face, and he jumps. "Wh— What is that?"

The spiral seems to be growing with each rotation, throwing off more light and even emitting a small sound as it turns. It's a high-pitched noise that is barely perceptible.

"I don't know . . . but it's cool, right?" I say, inching my foot closer. For some reason, I am not scared at all. For some reason, I feel like I should get even closer to investigate.

Ben grabs my arm.

"But it could be like a portal to another world or something," I say. "We need to check it out."

It appears to be a whirlpool, about a foot in diameter, circling and circling its light faster and faster. Like something out of *Star Trek* . . . or even a dream. *Maybe a rip in the fabric of space-time.*

Ben shakes his head, still staring at the thing. It's like he can't move, he's so shocked.

So the girl decides to lean down instead. As she does, the noise gets both higher and louder, and she has to plug her ears. It is a metallic scream, an electronic pin plucking her eardrum. But from this angle, she can see that the expanding spiral has depth, that although it is located on the forest floor, it looks like it leads to . . . someplace else? She brings her face closer to it, and her brother's grip on her arm gets stronger. She squints. "I—I can see something," she says. "I mean, someone. I see someone in there!" There is a blurry head, and a pair of ears, and two eyes. It's like they are shimmering in front of me, about to surface out of water.

She looks back at Ben, and he is shaking his head.

I look into the spiral deeply, and I see myself peering back at me. I mean . . . not myself precisely, but someone who looks exactly like me. It's like she is me and she isn't. She's got a scar above her left eye and I don't, and she's wearing clothes I would never wear, a bright red short-sleeve jumper, but other than that she looks just like me. And she seems like she is peering into a mirror or something. *Who's there?* she's asking. *Who is that?* She brings her face closer, and I reach my hand toward her, toward the center of the pulsating spiral.

"No!" Ben yells, and pulls at me, but it is too late. I touch the spiral and a giant spark goes off. It feels like an electrical current goes through my body, and the spiral starts sputtering and spitting. It turns on its side, and the escalating high-pitched noise is all-encompassing for a minute, making me feel like my head might explode. Then there is a small popping noise, and it is gone.

I blink. I reach out to where the spiral was only a moment before, but now it is only dirt. A stray leaf from a birch above languidly rides the air down, and lands where the spiral was.

I punch at the ground. "What?" But the ground is silent. It yields nothing.

I turn to Ben, desperation in my eyes. "Where did it go?"

He shakes his head. I can tell that he's glad it's gone.

"Come back!" I yell into the ground. "Come back!" But nothing happens. "Did you see her?" I ask Ben. She had my eyes: bright, and questioning.

Ben looks confused.

"Did you see the other me on the other side of the spiral?"

"N-no," he says.

I jump up, and stomp around the circle. "Okay, so it went away," I say. "If it went away, though, it's sure to be back sometime. And then we can study it. Find out what it's all about. Figure out who that other me is on the other side." It's like my muscles are powered with rubber or something. I can't seem to stop myself from bouncing off of things. I feel superpowered, like I sucked up all the energy from inside that spiral.

Ben is looking at me funny. He cocks his head to the side, and a red-haired curl falls over his eye. "Shan, are you okay?"

I throw my arm around him and hug his shoulders. "I'm fine, Ben. I'm fine," I say. "We just need to investigate. To solve this mystery, okay? Bit by bit."

He nods slowly, digesting my words. Not completely trusting me, because he knows there is a catch. With me, there is always a catch.

Moving out of the hug, I hold him at arm's length away from me, maintaining his glance. "But we can't tell anyone about this, okay?"

He looks unconvinced. He shifts his weight from right foot to left, then begins to fiddle with his fingers. It's something he does when he gets nervous, something bothers him, or I think maybe he has a weird thought. The last part of the ritual is that he brings his fingers to his mouth and touches them gently on his lips. He starts to lift his hand toward his mouth, but I grab it instead.

"It's not a good idea until we have more information, okay?" I lower his hand back down to his side. "Okay?"

He looks down at the ground. "Shan, I think we should talk to a grown-up about this. That was kind of . . . scary."

I shake my head. "If we tell a grown-up, they will think we're crazy, and also never let us back here. And then we'll really never find out what this whole thing's about."

Ben is still staring at the ground, kicking at the dirt.

"Right?" I press him. If I press him long enough, I know I will get my way.

He finally relents, and meets my glance.

"Right?"

He nods slowly. And I hug him.

Shannon is ten.

IT IS MIDDAY ON A SWELTERING SUMMER AFTERNOON, the humidity so thick you can barely hold on to anything, for the sweat. The spiral has not appeared for months, although I still check the woods every single day. Bobbi, my best friend who lives down the street and whose parents are far more permissive than mine, bikes over to our house after lunch to see if I want to swim at the neighborhood pool.

"Dad, can I go?" Shannon asks in a small voice, hoping to placate her father. He is mowing the lawn and obviously overheated, all of which does not bode well for his answer. She wishes her mother were home, because she is far more pliable with requests like this, but she left early that morning for a long shift at the hospital.

My father turns off the mower and wipes his brow. He squints at me, takes in Bobbi beside me. She has bulky blue glasses and thick brown hair that always seems to be tangled. Like me, she couldn't care less about her appearance. My parents have always liked Bobbi but resent the amount of time I spend at her house. They subscribe wholeheartedly to the solidly Midwestern ideal of the nuclear family being the solid unit of intimacy in all communities—something which will rankle and trouble our relationship in the decades to come. "What?" my dad asks irritably.

The girl shuffles her flip-flop, and looks up at her friend, who is frowning, perched atop her turquoise Schwinn. "Can I go down to the pool with Bobbi?"

Jim Gibney sighs. "You were just down there this morning, right?"

Shannon nods, seeing where this is going. A knot forms in her throat. She wants to tell her father how she and Bobbi have devised a game in which one person collects a bunch of invisible underwater gnomes and the other has to stack them carefully into some kind of pattern and then give clues to the other about what kind of pattern it is. She searches to find the words to explain that they promised each other they would go back and conclude the game after lunch, that it is imperative lest the gnomes disintegrate into the water, but the words elude me.

"No, I don't think you need to go back down there now. It's getting late," says Dad. Then he moves to pull the starter string on the lawn mower again.

I jump toward him, startling him. "But, Dad, it's only two o'clock! It's hours before the pool closes."

Dad's mouth settles into a tight thin line, which always means that his decision is made. Then he starts the mower again and pushes it over our too-high grass.

Shannon turns away from him, disgusted. The knot in her throat moves down into her stomach and begins to roil. She sticks out her tongue and makes her eyes googly to Bobbi, who laughs easily. Bobbi gets off her bike, and they both walk to the edge of the driveway, where the sound of the mower does not overpower their voices.

"Sorry," Bobbi says.

Shannon shrugs, then looks down at her feet. It isn't fair. But what can she do about it? Nothing. And she worries that if she speaks about it now, she will start crying.

"Okay, so see you later . . . ?" Bobbi says awkwardly, slinging her swim bag back over her shoulder, and getting on her bike.

I nod and wave her off. As she rides down the street, her long white legs pedaling languidly, I resist the urge to run after her all the way to the pool. There is no reason I should be bored out of my mind in this heat when I could be cooling off with Bobbi. I turn around and stare at my father, hatefully. He is still pushing the mower back and forth across the lawn, breathing heavily and deliberately, it seems to me, oblivious to my anger. I storm across the end of the driveway toward the front door, deciding to get myself situated for the next episode of *Robotech*, which is starting in approximately twenty-three minutes.

The brown minivan my parents use to haul my brothers and me to music lessons and soccer games and family gatherings is parked in the driveway, as usual. As I pass it, I notice how incredibly dirty it has become—completely covered in a layer of dust. I glance at my father, who looks like he is making his second to last turn around the lawn with the mower, his back toward me. Then I stick out my index finger and write on the side of the van in big block letters: "I HATE MY FAMILY."

The girl steps back for a moment to inspect her work, and she is surprised to find that she is pleased. In fact, a small smile spreads across her face when she reads the words she has written. "I hate my family," she whispers. Then she goes inside.

Mosquitoes buzz in the night air. It is nine fifteen, and I am a little tired, so the noise and movement keep me awake. We kids were already in bed when my mom stormed in and roused each of us, demanding that we come with her outside, onto the driveway.

Across the street, our neighbor Margie waves to us as she walks her garbage pail to the end of her driveway. No one waves back.

"Who wrote this?" Mom demands. She has lined up me and Jon and Ben beside the van, and points at the words etched in dirt across the side.

Ben peers at me from underneath his tangled red mane, clearly worried. Jon stares off into the night sky, at something only he can see. I shiver as a slight evening wind hits the hair on my forearms.

Mom fixes her tired blue eyes on me, and I see tiny wisps of blond hair that have escaped her ponytail sometime during her twelve-hour shift at the neonatal intensive care unit. "Shannon, was it you?"

My stomach plunges, and my right hand balls itself into a tight fist.

"Maybe somebody came out in the night and wrote it," Ben says, ever the peacemaker. "Like a kid in the neighborhood or something."

My mother crosses her arms in front of her chest tightly.

On the other side of me, Jon looks irritated. "Look, can we go in now? This is embarrassing."

I stifle a guffaw. Like my older brother is ever embarrassed of anything. He orders me and Ben around like we are his servants when Mom and Dad are still at work after school and is constantly taking apart and putting together various contraptions that he says will one day *do something.* All his teachers say he is *A Math Genius.* He doesn't even seem to notice, like I do, when we are at the library or grocery store, and people are looking at us quizzically, like, *What is this skinny little Black girl doing in this white family?*

"No," says Mom. "Not until I get some answers."

I allow myself to gaze longingly at the garage door. My bike, my favorite bike of all time, the Huffy Sweet Thunder, is parked inside, on the other side of the door. It is pink and white, has sturdy pedals so I can stand up or sit down when I am racing, and best of all, a big, thick seat so my bony butt won't start to ache. I close my eyes, and can almost see myself spinning through the neighborhood, down Terhune, across Brandywine, up Yost, my face soaking up all the sun.

"Shannon," Mom says to me, suddenly close up. "Why did you do it?"

My eyes fly open, and inside my fists my fingers are hard stones. "I never said I did it!" I was trying to not let myself be provoked, but I have failed. The words are out of my mouth before I can stop them. "Why do you always think it's me?"

My mother's eyes are wet around the edges, her face ragged with exhaustion. She takes a step back from me and shakes her head.

"Mom, it could be someone else. Like the person who stole our bikes last summer," says Ben.

Mom just ignores Ben and keeps looking at me. I think she is just sad.

"Can't you just tell me?" she asks, in a small voice. "I don't know why you won't talk to me anymore . . ."

Something inside me that's been clenched all this time breaks then, and I feel tears behind my eyes that I didn't even know were there. "I was mad," I say in a small voice. "I didn't mean it."

Beside me, Jon shakes his head. "So bogus," he says, under his breath. But I can hear him.

"Shut up!"

"You should shut up," he counters. "You're the reason we're out here."

"Both of you, enough!" Mom yells.

Jon and I glare at each other, but we shut our mouths.

Beside me, Ben takes my hand, and I let him.

"Shannon, why were you mad?" she asks me, trying to keep her voice level.

"I was mad at Dad," I say, trying to answer respectfully. "For not letting me go to the pool with Bobbi. I didn't mean it." And I am serious—I really *didn't* mean it. I know for sure I don't hate my family; I love them. And the look Mom is giving me now . . . Why would I ever want *that* on my conscience?

Mom nods, pursing her lips. She looks away, but I can still see one or two tears fall. Once, when I was four, Ben was three, and Jon was six, Mom was home with all of us and got so exhausted that she sat out front on the porch and just started crying. When we found her there, we hugged her tight, and felt so bad for running around and screaming and not listening and making her feel that way. She hugged us back, and told us that it wasn't our fault, that she was just so tired, and that she was sorry for crying like that. I remember that she and Dad had a serious late-night conversation after that, and she went to nursing school shortly afterward. It never happened again.

"I think . . . ," she says now, "I think I will see if I can go in a little late tomorrow, and we will go to the park tomorrow and work at the garden." She tries to smile. "Wouldn't that be fun?"

I nod. I want to run to her and hug her, but my feet are stuck hard to the ground for some reason.

"We really haven't had enough family time together lately. I think that would be good." She wipes her nose. "Get back in bed, okay?"

Jon doesn't have to be told twice. He runs to the house, every movement laced with agitation.

But Ben lingers, still holding my hand, trying to comfort me.

"Okay, Mom," I say in a small voice. "I'm sorry." But the words don't really mean anything—I sense it immediately. And I know she feels it, too, with her blotchy face, wiped clean of tears.

Bobbi and I huddle together on the cool fake leather bench inside my family's pop-up camper. It is rolled up on a rocky strip next to the house, a handy storage area my parents have created. They open it up to let it air out after any camping trip that involves rain—which seems to be most of them for some reason—and we kids are allowed to play inside. I don't know how long Bobbi and I have before my brothers and their friends invade our hidden space with their Dragonmaster game, so I tell her we should practice the new song we have written. They will, of course, try to spoil it if they hear it.

S.G. and B.C., S.G. and B.C.
We would like to say (we would like to say, yes we would)
We could sing all day (we could sing all day, yes we could)
S.G. and B.C., S.G. and B.C.

We giggle conspiratorially at our craftiness. We like the song because it emphasizes and contrasts our initials, and has a ridiculous,
childlike tune. But the big secret about the song is that it purposefully
elides the most interesting part of our names, the curious detail that
cemented our best friendship when we first met on this street when we
were six: We share a middle name. I am Shannon Elaine Gibney, and
Bobbi is Roberta Elaine Chase. Bobbi's full initials, REC, are the same
as her father's. Although Bobbi doesn't fight, she will seriously con-
template doing so if you call her "Roberta." She is adamant about her
distaste for the name and has gone by "Bobbi" since she could speak.
Like each of us, she is a co-creation of her own personal wants, desires,
aversions and histories, and her parents'. They wanted her to have a
formal name that would stand up well to high academic success, and
Dr. Roberta Chase had a nice ring to it. But they didn't think it would
wear well for everyday use growing up. Bobbi agreed.

"Hey, should we make a book to go with the song?" I ask her excit-
edly.

Bobbi shrugs. "Sure." She is not *not* excited, but she is also not excited, so I decide to file it away for a possible future project. She maneuvers off the bench and stands up in the small space of the camper's main
walkway. "It's getting late. We need to get your stuff for the sleepover."

I clap my hands. I had almost forgotten! My parents actually easily agreed to me having dinner and sleeping over at Bobbi's house,
something which is usually a battle for some reason. "Excellent!" I say,
squeezing myself off the bench. "I think I just need my nightgown,
toothbrush, and clothes for tomorrow." I circle her elbow in mine, and

we walk awkwardly to the camper door. We open it, and my brothers and their friends jump back on the other side.

"Hey! Watch it!" Jon yells.

We laugh, and stumble down the three camper steps to the ground.

"We were coming to see if you were up for a Dragonmaster tournament," says Ben. His eyes sparkle with anticipation. "We could have teams of two! Winner gets these!" He shoves his palm in our faces, and opens it to reveal a bunch of red, green, purple, white, yellow, black, and orange gems.

Bobbi and I look at each other, shake our heads, and laugh. "No way," we say. Then we walk past them.

"Oh, come on, guys!" Ben says to our backs. "It'll be fun!"

But it's no use—we can already see ourselves seated at Bobbi's dinner table, eating spaghetti, and watching *The Muppet Movie* again afterward. "Sorry," I say, but it's clear in my tone I am not.

S.G. and B.C., S.G. and B.C., we sing under our breath until we are out of the yard.

Erin Powers is twelve.

ESSIE AND ERIN pace the steps of the Utica Public Library. Or rather, Erin paces and Essie watches anxiously.

"What did he say?" Essie asks. She leans against the railing, mittened hands holding her elbows.

Erin shakes her head. "Nothing," she says. "Nothing of use to us, anyway."

Erin's hands are burrowed into her light-brown winter jacket, now way too small for her after three years. It barely covers her stomach, and the skin on her forearms is exposed where the jacket ends. She clomps her feet in the moon boots that Aunt Bridget gave her as an early Christmas present this year.

Essie studies her friend carefully. Erin has always been thin, but lately, as she's become more obsessed with searching for her father, she has not been eating very much. She will have her regular cereal for breakfast and maybe some fruit for a snack during the day, but she often resorts to a peanut butter and jelly sandwich for dinner, while she pores over this document or that one. Erin's mother, Essie knows, is passed out most nights and won't check on her. That's why Essie invites her over for dinner at her house all the time. But Erin has been declining lately, saying she wants to look into this lead or that one.

"But what did he *say*?" Essie presses her.

Erin sighs, and turns on her heel once more. "He said what everyone always says: That he's probably dead by now. That he was a lost soul and had mental health problems . . . whatever that means. And that he was very sorry, but that he couldn't release any information to anyone who's not immediate family, and certainly not a minor." With that last bit of information, Erin looks Essie right in the eyes, so that she cannot avoid the pain in their depths.

And Essie feels it, the dull cut of bureaucratic words that are just "policy" to a government worker, but razor-sharp to an unacknowledged and maybe even unknown daughter searching for her father. Essie's own family is a welter of uncles and aunts and cousins, coming and going from Mexico and New York and various places between, along with her five siblings and constantly-in-motion parents. They irritate her, they *always* irritate her, but they are *hers* and she is theirs, she knows their stories, and those she doesn't know she basically knows how to get access to, and nothing will ever change that. Being friends with Erin has shown her the gift of that, even in its complexity and weight. She sees what it does to Erin to not know—the hunger for the filled-in blank spaces—and it hurts her. Essie wishes more than anything that she could fix it, but since she knows she can't, she just sits in the ick of it with her friend. And sometimes, like now, they wade through it. Over and over again.

Essie walks over and envelops Erin in a hug. Erin is taller than Essie, with sharper edges, and she is less inclined to touching of any sort, but she allows it. Besides her uncle Jim, who only occasionally hugs her, Essie is really the only person Erin will allow to get close to her, physically or otherwise.

"But you *are* immediate family," Essie says quietly.

Erin shrugs. "I can't prove it," she says. "To anyone."

Essie frowns, holding Erin at arm's length. A mother pulls her reluctant child past them. He looks about five, and is holding on to the railing with everything he's got. He kicks her when she tries to disengage his hands, and she yelps. "Felix!" she yells. The little boy grins, and runs back down the steps. The mother hobbles after him, working her way around us. "Sorry," she says as she passes by.

"No problem," says Erin. Then she turns to Essie and smiles unexpectedly, lighting up the walkway.

Essie smiles back. She can never resist Erin's energy when she puts it on her—it's why she's gotten in so much trouble through the years.

"My mom would hit me for sure if I tried something like that," says Erin.

Essie's smile fades. She doesn't like to hear about Patricia hitting Erin. "My brother says you should just hire a private investigator at this point," she says, changing the subject.

"What's that?" Erin asks.

"It's like a cop who you pay to do what you say," says Essie. "To look into things, to dig up information and stuff."

"Oh," says Erin.

"Except they're not a cop."

Erin nods. It has started snowing, and a few flakes land on her nose. She brushes them off. "Sounds expensive," she says.

"Dinero es Dios en este país," says Essie. "That's what my papa always says." She locks her arm in Erin's. "Come on, let's get out of here."

The two girls walk down the stairs, snow falling faster around and on them. They start a brisk pace, heading back home. Essie already knows she will convince Erin to stay for supper.

Erin gets home late, after dinner, dessert, and homework at Essie's. "Mom?" she asks as she walks through the front door.

"In here," her mom calls from her bedroom, her language slurred. She probably had another extended date with Tracey and ended up drinking till they passed out again.

Erin sighs, and heads to the bathroom to wash her face and brush her teeth for bed. She squints in the mirror, inspecting her skin, which looks good except for some blackheads that seem to be proliferating on her nose. She sighs and takes her toothbrush out of the cup by the sink. When she looks into the mirror again, she sees a bright white spiral of light. "Oh my God!" She drops her toothbrush into the sink. The spiral is turning and getting bigger with each revolution. Sparks are starting to fly, and an electrical hum is slowly building. Erin kicks up her knees and squeals. *I knew I wasn't dreaming! And now it's back.* As the spiral expands, Erin sees a shimmering tunnel appear within its depths, and before she can even register a reaction, another tunnel appears beside it. The first tunnel leads back to the woods she saw the last time, but the girl who looks like her is not there. The second tunnel looks like it leads to a kitchen, where two little white kids are running around, and a light-skinned Black mom is trying to get their attention. It's all very blurry, like looking through a kaleidoscope. Although the woman's back is to her, she looks very familiar. The tunnel to the woods shudders for a moment, and then pops out a small passageway. Erin gasps. There, on the other side of a tunnel branching off from the other tunnels, is her father. She doesn't know how she knows it is him; she just does. With a striped T-shirt and something bigger than a cigarette hanging from his lip. Talking to his friends and laughing. He has her forehead, or rather she has his, with its long, broad spread over and down across his nose. And his eyes, which sparkle with the same mischief as hers do.

She cups her hands and yells, "Dad!" into the tunnel in the mirror.

He looks around for a moment, confused, and peers toward her, squinting into the light. "Who's that?" she hears him say. "Shannon? That you?"

Erin's brow furrows. *Who's Shannon?* Then there are sparks, and then tunnel walls start vibrating. "No," says Erin. She steps about a foot away from the mirror so she can get a full view of the spiral. It is starting to expand and contract, expand and contract. "No!" she exclaims. She can just barely make out the outline of her dad's profile in the after-outline of the tunnel on the spiral. "Dad, don't go!" she yells.

And then there is a high-pitched popping noise, which she recognizes from two years ago, and the spiral shrinks to a dot.

"Dad!" she screams as the dot disappears back to where it came from.

She falls to the floor, defeated in the knowledge that it's gone now, and will only come back when it's ready. "I'll find you," she whispers, head in her hands. "I promise."

STATE OF CALIFORNIA
CERTIFICATION OF VITAL RECORD

COUNTY of SANTA CLARA
SAN JOSE, CALIFORNIA

CERTIFICATE OF DEATH
STATE OF CALIFORNIA   4300-08172   185

STATE FILE NUMBER | LOCAL REGISTRATION DISTRICT AND CERTIFICATE NUMBER

DECEDENT PERSONAL DATA

1A. NAME OF DECEDENT—FIRST	1B. MIDDLE	1C. LAST	2A. DATE OF DEATH (MONTH, DAY, YEAR)	2B. HOUR
Boisey	Winfred	COLLINS	December 20, 1981	2200

3. SEX	4. RACE	5. ETHNICITY	6. DATE OF BIRTH	7. AGE	IF UNDER 1 YEAR MONTHS DAYS	IF UNDER 24 HOURS HOURS MINUTES
M	Black		Nov. 4, 1946	35 YEARS		

8. BIRTHPLACE OF DECEDENT (STATE OR FOREIGN COUNTRY)	9. NAME AND BIRTHPLACE OF FATHER	10. NAME AND BIRTHPLACE OF MOTHER
MISS.	BOISEY COLLINS	ANNIE

11. CITIZEN OF WHAT COUNTRY	12. SOCIAL SECURITY NUMBER	13. MARITAL STATUS	14. NAME OF SURVIVING SPOUSE (IF WIFE, ENTER MAIDEN NAME)
U.S.A.		MARRIED	ERNESTINE MUSCHIK

15. PRIMARY OCCUPATION	16. NUMBER OF YEARS THIS OCCUPATION	17. EMPLOYER (IF SELF-EMPLOYED, SO STATE)	18. KIND OF INDUSTRY OR BUSINESS
Electronic Tec	8	G. E. Nuclear Co., S.J.	Electronics

RESIDENCE

19A. USUAL RESIDENCE—STREET ADDRESS (STREET AND NUMBER OR LOCATION)	19B.	19C. CITY OR TOWN
L.A. HILLS	511701	PALO ALTO

19D. COUNTY	19E. STATE	20. NAME AND ADDRESS OF INFORMANT — RELATIONSHIP
SANTA CLARA	CALIFORNIA	SPOUSE

PLACE OF DEATH 13

21A. PLACE OF DEATH	21B. COUNTY	SAME AS 19A
Santa Clara Valley Medical Center	Santa Clara	

21C. STREET ADDRESS (STREET AND NUMBER OR LOCATION)	21D. CITY OR TOWN	
751 S. Bascom Ave.	San Jose	

CAUSE OF DEATH

22. DEATH WAS CAUSED BY: (ENTER ONLY ONE CAUSE PER LINE FOR A, B, AND C)		24. WAS DEATH REPORTED TO CORONER?
IMMEDIATE CAUSE (A) Staphylococcal Pneumonia	APPROXIMATE INTERVAL BETWEEN ONSET AND DEATH	Yes
CONDITIONS, IF ANY, WHICH GAVE RISE TO THE IMMEDIATE CAUSE, STATING THE UNDERLYING CAUSE LAST. DUE TO, OR AS A CONSEQUENCE OF (B) Head Injury	16days	25. WAS BIOPSY PERFORMED? No
DUE TO, OR AS A CONSEQUENCE OF (C)		26. WAS AUTOPSY PERFORMED? Yes

23. OTHER CONDITIONS CONTRIBUTING BUT NOT RELATED TO THE IMMEDIATE CAUSE OF DEATH	27. WAS OPERATION PERFORMED FOR ANY CONDITION IN ITEMS 22 OR 23? TYPE OF OPERATION DATE
P 8120	No

PHYSICIAN'S OR CORONER'S CERTIFICATION

28A. I CERTIFY THAT DEATH OCCURRED AT THE HOUR, DATE AND PLACE STATED FROM THE CAUSES STATED. I ATTENDED DECEDENT SINCE	28B. PHYSICIAN—SIGNATURE AND DEGREE OR TITLE	28C. DATE SIGNED	28D. PHYSICIAN'S LICENSE NUMBER

INJURY INFORMATION

29. SPECIFY ACCIDENT, SUICIDE, ETC.	30. PLACE OF INJURY	31. INJURY AT WORK	32A. DATE OF INJURY (MONTH, DAY, YEAR)	32B. HOUR
Accident	Street	No	December 4, 1981	1512

33. LOCATION (STREET AND NUMBER OR LOCATION AND CITY OR TOWN)	34. DESCRIBE HOW INJURY OCCURRED (EVENTS WHICH RESULTED IN INJURY)
Alma St. at 7th ST. San Jose	Auto/Truck Driver of auto

CORONER'S USE ONLY

35A. I CERTIFY THAT DEATH OCCURRED AT THE HOUR, DATE AND PLACE STATED FROM THE CAUSES STATED, AS REQUIRED BY LAW I HAVE HELD AN INQUEST/INVESTIGATION	35B. CORONER—SIGNATURE AND DEGREE OR TITLE John E. Hauser, M.D.	35C. DATE SIGNED
Investigation	John E. Hauser M.D. 751 So. Bascom, San Jose	12-21-81

BURIAL

36. DISPOSITION	37. DATE (MONTH, DAY, YEAR)	38. NAME AND ADDRESS OF CEMETERY OR CREMATORY	39. EMBALMER'S LICENSE NUMBER AND SIGNATURE
	12-30-1981	RIVERSIDE NATIONAL CEM. RIVERSIDE,	4158

40. NAME OF FUNERAL DIRECTOR (OR PERSON ACTING AS SUCH)	41. LOCAL REGISTRAR	42. DATE ACCEPTED BY LOCAL REGISTRAR
REDWOOD CHAPEL		DEC 29 1981

STATE REGISTRAR | A. | B. | C. | D. | E. | F.

Boisey Collins' death certificate.

PART THREE

Time. Travel.

Speculation

IF: "The wormhole theory postulates that a theoretical passage through space-time could create shortcuts for long journeys across the universe;"

And If: "A wormhole (or Einstein-Rosen bridge) is a speculative structure linking disparate points in spacetime, and is based on a special solution of the Einstein field equations solved using a Jacobian matrix and determinant. A wormhole can be visualized as a tunnel with two ends, each at separate points in spacetime (i.e., different locations or different points of time) . . . A wormhole could connect extremely long distances such as a billion light years or more, short distances such as a few meters, different universes, or different points in time;"[1]

Then: Perhaps we may dare hope to find that reunion is just a wormhole between two points (mother and child, for example) on one distinct timeline?

---

1. Wormhole. (2022, June 29). In Wikipedia. https://en.wikipedia.org/wiki/Wormhole

1994.

From materials sent by the adoption agency to Shannon.

REUNION TIPS FOR TRIAD MEMBERS

1. Work together with adoptive parents and birthparents when planning a reunion. Make sure each triad member is aware of and comfortable with the plans being made.

2. Structure some time to be alone between each day's meetings. You will need time to process what has just occurred.

3. Keep a journal. Record your experiences and your feelings. This helps to diffuse the intensity which surrounds reunions.

4. Be aware of the broad range of feelings you are likely to experience. The following experiences are possible:

    1) A feeling of magnetism toward birthparent
    2) A "thirst" for information
    3) A need to touch each other-as if to prove this is truly happening.
    4) A feeling of loss and grief-a feeling of sadness over what could have been.
    5) A tendency to protect birthparent and adoptive parent.

5. Be aware and sensitive to the feelings of your birthparent. He/she may be emotionally overwhelmed at times.

6. Don't underestimate the power of this experience for each triad member.

7. You may feel possessive and controlling toward the reunion experience. Remember it is a triad experience.

8. Recognize it may be difficult to say good-bye and you may experience a fear of disconnection after each day's events. Plan for the next day and/or the next meeting with your birthparent. Having a date and time to reconnect if it's only by phone, will be reassuring.

9. Give yourself some time alone to reflect, to cry or to process each new bit of information you will receive from your birthparent. You may experience grief, loss, pain or anger during this time.

10. Be considerate of how frightening this reunion may be for adoptive parents. Praise their efforts and reassure them of your love at this time.

11. Share something personal with your birthparent-a special picture, a childhood locket, flowers or a special keepsake.

12. Enjoy and embrace this wonderful event-the completion of who you are. You may gain much more than you dared hope to find.

Letter from Patricia Powers to Shannon Gibney.

on a lighter note, continue to enjoy the Autumn beauty and your studies.

I do believe that you and I are soul, heart and lovingly eternally connected - that, as long as we continue to risk and embrace honest communication, that will be our resolution. I do want to say that if any of my curt verbalizations hurt you - I am sorry. Our diversity is one of our gifts. we found each other because we both risk and hunger for truth, certainly our truths will differ; I am just as certain that our differing truths will resolutely continue to unite us. Shannon, I love you; I have loved you since

you spoke to me so many years ago when I chose to listen to your yearning to be in this world.   (it was actually a scream to me)

this is happening for a reason. we both are meant to learn something here. we both are teachers too; according to principles of learning theory, (Based on Nursing Research), ~~I said~~ teaching will occur only when the teacher is open to learning ... (Based on 14 principles of learning theory).

I look forward to your visit - I hope we can go to Bookstore together, one day too I would love to show you and Eric

Letter from Patricia to Shannon.

Provincetown (must be warmer weather). Perhaps next Summer or following Summer.

Q: why didn't the witch have any children?

A: Because her husband had a crystal balls.

I know, I know; a really dumb childhood joke.

XOXO,

Love,

P.S. Hey eric, How about those yankees?

Letter from Patricia to Shannon, continued.

Unfortunately, I have no knowledge of your biological father's family history. I would however advise you to contact them to try to find out if there is a family history of breast cancer particularly in your biological grandmother. . . . I do believe that you and I are soul, heart and lovingly eternally connected—that, as long as we continue to risk and embrace honest communication, that will be our resolution. I do want to say that if any of my curt verbalizations hurt you—I am sorry. Our diversity is one of our gifts. We found each other because we both risk and hunger for truth. Certainly our truths will differ; I am just as certain that our differing truths will resolutely continue to unite us. Shannon, I love you; I have loved you since you spoke to me so many years ago when I chose to listen to your yearning to be in this world. (it was actually a scream to me)

This is happening for a reason. We both are meant to learn something here. We both are teachers too; according to principles of learning theory (based on nursing research), teaching will occur only when the teacher is open to learning . . . (Based on 14 principles of learning theory).

I look forward to your visit—I hope we can go to Bookstore together. One day too I would love to show you and Eric Provincetown (must be warmer weather). Perhaps next summer or following summer.

Q: Why didn't the witch have any children?
A: Because her husband had crystal balls.
I know, I know, a really dumb childhood joke.

xoxo,

Love,

Patricia

Patricia and Shannon at her home in Utica, NY, December 1994. First reunion meeting.

Shannon Gibney is nineteen.

"NO, NO. TURN LEFT!" I tell Bobbi, frantically peering at the mashed-up map in my hands. "I think Clinton is off of Newbury." Bobbi turns the steering wheel of the '89 Toyota Corolla that my parents have let us drive from Ann Arbor all the way out to Utica, a seven-and-a-half-hour journey across the U.S. and Canada that will ultimately end at my birth mother's, Patricia Powers', house.

"Okay, okay, yeah," I say, pointing ahead. "I can see the sign right up there."

Bobbi swats away my arm, blocking her view of the road. She grumbles something under her breath, and I grin. We have been best friends for thirteen years now, and although we often laugh as sisters, we can bicker like them, too. "I see it," she says irritably. She downshifts into second gear, and we rumble up the quiet suburban street. The houses are maybe sixty or seventy years old, sturdy single-family dwellings with small, snow-filled lawns. I have been to New York City, to drop my older brother Jon off at Columbia, but I have never ventured to this part of the state before. I can't quite pinpoint how it feels different from the Midwest, but it definitely does. There is a kind of hum underneath everything, an electricity that animates this small, working-class town, that I don't feel back in Ann Arbor.

Bobbi is a sophomore at Rensselaer Polytechnic Institute, in Troy, New York, where she is studying environmental science. When I told her I had found out that my birth mom lived in Utica, the first thing she said was "Oh my God, that's like an hour and a half from Troy!

We have to visit." Then she caught herself, and her breath. "I mean . . . if you want to. If you decide you want to visit, I'll go with you." I told her I would think about it.

Patricia's house is modest, a two-story bungalow with a small porch in front. Yellow trim lines the quaint brick exterior. "Cute," I say as Bobbi pulls the car up the slightly inclined driveway. She nods in agreement.

We have been in the car for more than two hours since our last pit stop, and I know that Bobbi's long legs are killing her. She practically leaps out of the driver's seat, and stretches for a moment on the driveway. I am more taciturn, realizing all at once that we are here. We are *here*, which means that in just a moment, I will gather myself, walk down the concrete pathway to the front door, and knock. And the woman on the other side will be the one who gave birth to me. And relinquished me shortly thereafter. The woman I have been conversing with weekly on the phone these past two months, as well as trading letters with. When Bobbi and I had determined that we would, in fact, make the trip, I realized that we would need money for gas and other incidentals like food. My work-study job at the college would not cover these expenses, so I reluctantly acknowledged that I would need to ask Patricia to cover them if I was going to go. When I did, she did not react well, saying that she would have to think about it, and hung up on me shortly afterward. Later, she called me back to apologize, saying that she had been taken advantage of many times in her life, and was overcautious because of it. But after talking about it with her partner, Josephine, she saw that it was a reasonable request, and one that she could grant.

I lean my head against the cool car window, its icy edges calming my increasingly hot skin. I think about my parents back home in Ann Arbor, who were incredibly hurt when I told them about the search, and my brothers, who don't understand why I need to do it at all (if

I'm honest, I'm not sure I do, either). And yet, they have loaned me their car, and have somehow found a way to listen to my stories of non-identifying information, Central Registries, and now, reunion.

There's a sharp tap on the window, and I'm broken from my reverie. Bobbi pulls back her gloved hand, and asks me if I'm okay, through the muffled glass. I nod, grafting an awkward smile across my face. Apparently satisfied, Bobbi steps under the porch awning. Then she digs for something in her purse, waiting for me. I undo my seat belt, and prepare to open the door, but when I look past her, I see the strangest thing.

Two houses down, a young woman runs down the front steps of a house. She is bundled in a brown jacket that looks much too small for her, and a knitted red hat that looks like a misshapen mushroom. But it's the way she walks that catches my attention: studied and forceful. Like she is determined to get something from the world. *Her walk is my own.* I don't know how I know it, but I do. I push the door open quickly, and stand up, the shock of the cold piercing every cell in my body. *Could she be . . . her? The girl on the other side of the wormhole I saw all those years ago?* I don't know where this thought comes from, but it appears and stays, defiant. The girl is walking quickly toward an old, rusted yellow VW Beetle parked at the curb. A girl who looks much shorter, and Latina, sits behind the wheel. When she hears my car door slam, the girl who is me and not me turns. When her eyes meet mine, they widen in surprise, and I know she is thinking the same thing as me: *What the fuck is going on? Is that me?* Because she has my face. Or I have hers. Or something. Maybe Patricia had twins? Maybe we were separated at birth, and this girl, my sister, is being raised by family here, while I was given up? I rub my eyes, because I want to make sure I'm awake, not dreaming, and I hear the girl in the VW shout something in Spanish through the open shotgun seat window.

"Shannon," Bobbi is saying to me.

I force myself to focus on the clear, familiar sound of her voice, grounding me. Reluctantly, I break my glance with my twin, and address Bobbi. Her brown eyes are filled with worry.

"D-did you see that?" I ask.

"See what?" Bobbi asks, her face a mask of confusion.

"Look! Right there!" I say, pointing to the girl who was frozen on the steps only moments before. But she is not there anymore. I gasp, as the rusted VW Beetle chugs past us, its windows all rolled up and foggy. It's impossible to see anyone inside.

"That *is* an old car," says Bobbi. "I kind of can't believe it still runs."

"But I saw her! I know it was her," I say, and before I know what's happening, I am running out into the street, chasing the car. "Hey! Hey, stop!" I yell.

I know it's her. I know it's me.

Bobbi runs out to the middle of the street where I am and grabs my arm. This stops me from running. "Hey," she says as I slam into her. "Stop."

I look past her shoulder, at the spot of yellow that finally turns the corner and is gone. I sigh, deflated.

"What just happened?" Bobbi asks.

I have never told her about the wormhole, the other me on the other side, or the second incident, with my birth father. I have wanted to, many times, but I was worried about what she would think of me, and to be honest, I was wondering if any of it had actually happened, after all these years. "I . . . thought I saw someone," I tell her weakly.

She lets go of my arm, and takes a step back. "Someone . . . ?"

I sigh again. "Someone I've seen before."

She looks at me strangely, like she doesn't know who I am.

I look down at my feet, and dig for words. "Someone who reminds me . . ." *She's gone now. But maybe I can find her again, especially if she is so close.* I look back up at Bobbi, her big clear plastic glasses reflecting the late-afternoon sun. I catch a flicker of movement out of the corner of my eye. I turn and see two women, pushing a curtain aside and peering at us curiously, in the middle of the street. My face reddens. "Forget it. Let's go," I tell Bobbi. Then I turn on my heel, and stride up the walk with as much confidence as I can muster. This was not the way I wanted to meet her.

I stand in front of a simple oak door. A Christmas wreath, decorated with holly, and red ribbon, and a wood carving of children on a sled, hangs in the middle. My heart thwacking like a hammer in my chest, I raise my right hand and knock three times. Once I do, Bobbi is beside me, standing tall as always, hands clasped behind her back. She is nervous, too, I realize.

The door flies open abruptly, and then she is there. An average-sized white woman with short blond hair that stops just above her ears, and bangs that have been curled specially and sprayed in place. Her nose is thin and long; I can see that I inherited it. Her eyes are cautious, which I expected, but I can also see that at one point they were easygoing, overflowing with wonder at the world. But life has done its work on her, and she is different now.

"Hi," I say. It feels idiotic, but it's what you say.

"Hi," she says, and her voice is low, gravelly. I have heard it on the phone these last few months, but somehow it didn't seem so heavy to me over the line. More than twenty years later, after she has died from something called anaplastic carcinoma, I will learn that she smokes two packs a day, but hides it from me the whole time we are in reunion. Now, however, not having much exposure to smoking or smokers, I don't make the connection.

"We made it," I say. The wind whips up around Bobbi and me, and I shiver.

"You're taller than I expected," she says abruptly.

I laugh. I am five feet seven inches, but Bobbi is almost six feet tall, and when your best friend is so much taller than you, you don't think of yourself as tall.

She keeps staring, taking me in.

A thick white woman with curly blond hair and a welcoming smile steps from behind her. "Well, let them in, Patricia!" she says with a laugh.

"Oh my God, what am I thinking? I'm not," says Patricia, and she gestures for us to come inside.

We do, and the warmth of the house envelops us, as does Christmas music, playing on the stereo in the next room. I look around and see that the whole house is covered in holiday decorations, from the manger ornaments on the hearth, to the gingerbread men stickers on the windows, to the plastic holly and ivy taped to the molding.

Patricia's eyes follow my own, noting everything that catches my attention. "We're a little obsessed with Christmas in this house," she says, laughing nervously. "You know, your Irish Catholic roots and all."

I want to say that my adoptive family is Irish Catholic, too, and we don't even have a fourth of this stuff up around the holidays, but I don't. Instead, I smile, and tell my birth mother that she has a beautiful home. Over phone conversations and our correspondence these past few months, she has revealed to me that she spent seventeen years of her life as an alcoholic, and just barely made it out of the black hole of addiction alive. I know that some part of the black hole's pull originated from her family's inability to accept her lesbianism, because she has told me so. I know that another part of its pull has to do with losing me, because she hasn't told me so. In any case, knowing all of this makes the bright red-and-black stair runner, antique light fixtures, and solid oak paneling all the more impressive. These past few years of sobriety, education, and work have been the best of her life, she said. And then, too, she found love. I want to ask how she and Josephine got together, but I have a feeling that I won't find a way to do so during this visit—it would still be too awkward.

"Follow me," she says, walking down a narrow hallway, and then turning right. She opens the door to a small bedroom, and walks in. The room is modest, with a twin bed and nightstand beside it. A painting of a blue jay hangs on the wall. "This will be your room while you're here." She steps to the side so I can squeeze by her with my duffel, and set it on the bed. "Look okay?" I can hear how nervous she is in her tone. I still can't quite wrap my mind around the fact that she is *my mother*. An aunt, maybe, but mother? It is a truth from another timeline to me.

"It's beautiful," I say. "It's perfect." It *will* be cozy in here, especially under the covers at night, and I am glad I will have my own space to decompress after what I'm sure will be some fairly intense discussions with family. It will be a dense three-day visit, but it's what I want. Bobbi's boyfriend Dustin's family lives in Utica, too, so she will be staying with them.

Patricia and Josephine invite Bobbi to stay for dinner with us, but she declines, saying that Dustin is waiting for her. There is a brightness to her eyes, and I can see she is excited to see him.

"You'll be okay?" she asks, whispering in my ear in the foyer.

Patricia and Josephine stand just a few feet away. I nod, then hug her hard.

"Okay," she says breathlessly. "Call if you need anything."

I nod again.

"You have the number. Anything at all."

I smile, waving her away. Then she is out the door, and I hear the sound of an engine starting, the gears of the car shifting to reverse. In a moment she is gone, and I am alone for the first time with my mother and her partner.

———————

As it turns out, Josephine is *Italian* Italian, and after a delicious dinner she cooks for us of manicotti with sausage and peppers, I fall into an exhausted sleep in the guest room. I sleep so deeply, in fact, that I barely hear the delicate knock at my door around ten a.m.

"Shannon?" Patricia's gravelly voice whispers from the other side. "Are you awake?"

I open my eyes, remembering where I am and why, and sit straight up in bed. My eyes turn to the small nondescript clock on the night-stand, and I am embarrassed to realize that I have slept for twelve hours straight. My birth mother's first impression of me will be one of sloth.

"Yes," I say groggily. "Getting up now."

Half an hour and a shower later, I am sitting at their modest oak dining room table, a spread of fruit danishes, yogurt, and cereal before me.

Patricia stands at the stove, pouring hot water into a mug for green tea. Outside, the snow is piling up on the sidewalks and outside of win-dows. It has been snowing steadily since the early morning.

"Better get all insulated with food for today," she says. She pulls the tea bag string and wraps it around the mug handle. Then she brings it to me. The steam off the top is both warming and calming. "Gonna be a cold one."

"Negative twenty with windchill," says Josephine, taking a sip of her coffee.

I lean over my mug of tea, eager to take a sip.

"Careful!" Patricia says, startling me.

I jump in my seat.

This is what is has been like the whole time we have been talking on the phone, writing, and now visiting in person: me trying to get closer, more intimate, inching toward the blank details that brought me into existence, and her anxiously trying to protect me at the slightest provo-cation, physical or otherwise.

"It's really hot," she says, somewhat abashed.

I nod, and instead inch toward the tea incrementally, blowing on it. I sit on my hands, so she will not be worried I might burn them. I want to ask her about my birth father, but I don't know how. After much investigation, Bobbi and I found his death certificate last summer. Cause of death was injuries he sustained from a high-speed police chase in Palo Alto, California, when I was six. I want to know if Patricia knows anything about that, if she kept in contact with him at all through the years. If he even knew I existed.

"Your parents," Patricia says slowly, sitting down across from me. "What do they think of all this?" Her eyes are worried, and she fiddles with a half-eaten strawberry on her plate.

I shrug. "Fine," I say. I see my parents turn away from me, attempting to mask their hurt at my excitement at receiving a letter with information on Patricia inside. I wince. "I mean, it's not easy or anything. But they know I need to do it."

Patricia smiles ruefully. "Right," she says. "You seem like a person who does what they need to do, regardless of the consequences. I was like that once, too." She is looking out the window at the portly, bundled-up neighbor shoveling her walk. I have been studiously watching everything and everyone outside, looking for Other Me and her friend, but I haven't seen them at all. "But then I guess I found out how bad the consequences can be . . ."

I take a tentative sip of my tea, and Patricia is right, it is very hot. It burns my tongue a little, and I resolve to take smaller sips from now on. In my mind, I can see the girl who is not me, who might have been me, who is me, sitting inside her house, on her sofa just two doors down, and the words suddenly gallop out before I can catch them. "Hey, is there a Black girl who looks a lot like me, who lives close by?"

Patricia and Josephine stare at me, clearly surprised by the turn the conversation has taken.

I draw back from them, feeling suddenly embarrassed. "I mean, I saw her run out the door of her house when Bobbi and I pulled up yesterday, and I was just surprised that she looked so much like me . . ."

I am the one who is surprised next, at Patricia's full-throated laugh. "My mom, your grandma Powers, lives two doors down, actually! That's so funny that you noticed it yesterday."

Josephine eyes me carefully, then addresses Patricia. "She probably saw Mom's new home health aide. She just started last week. She's excellent."

Patricia finally commits to eating the rest of her strawberry. "Excellent," she agrees. "What's her name again?"

Josephine's brow furrows. "I can't remember . . . Dana? Danai? Something like that . . . some unusual kind of name."

Patricia nods. "But she's half-Black, not Black," she says, the words flowing out of her way too easily. "Just like you."

I almost choke on the perfectly crispy apple turnover I'm chewing. This "you're only half-Black" refrain is an idea so odious to me that I jettisoned it years ago. Yes, I am mixed, and yes, that matters, but by now I am clear that mixed is just another kind of Black. And that it certainly doesn't work the other way, with white. I wonder what my Black father, and my Black relatives on that side, would have to say about this.

"If you have one drop of Black blood in you in this country, the government sees you as Black," I say, in as even a tone as I can muster. "*Everyone* sees you as Black."

Patricia's face screws up into the mask of white defensiveness that is all too familiar to me, even at nineteen. "Everyone except your white mother," she says icily.

I swallow the food in my mouth.

Josephine has gotten up to put her dishes in the sink.

"It erases me when you say that," she continues. "Which feels terrible, because I already feel erased."

I don't have anything to say to that, so I just keep on chewing. I wonder if it was such a good idea to come all the way out here after all. I wonder if there are some family knots you just can't untie. Years later, recounting the story to my Black girlfriends, they will ask, *But she knows she fucked a Black man, right?* And we will laugh and laugh . . . But in this moment, all I feel is alone. That is probably why, thinking I have nothing to lose at this point, I ask her about my birth father.

Patricia scowls, and there is also fear on her face. Josephine comes back from the sink, and sits down beside her.

"What do you want to know about him?"

I shrug, feeling completely detached from her emotions for a moment, and therefore, free. "I want to know everything." I can see him again, nine years ago, on the side of the road, peering at me like a ghost coming through a portal.

Patricia stands up, suddenly, angry. "Well, I don't know everything, Shannon," she says crossly. "In fact, I only know a little. A very little."

Then she looks back at me, my yearning, and sleepy eyes, and I see something in her yield. "Okay, this is what I know." She sits down beside me at the table. Josephine takes her hand. "We met at a disco, at the airport base not far from here. He was in the Air Force. We talked about Detroit and music. We were both into Dylan and Joan Baez . . ."

I stare at her expectantly, desperately grasping at any small bit of information she can give me. I stand up and grab a pad of paper and pen on the kitchen counter, sit back down, and start taking notes. "Go on."

This brings Patricia back to herself. "He had a steel guitar," she says. "I would write lyrics, and we would sing together."

I laugh. I cannot picture it. She is too stiff, too war-torn from surviving all the things life has done to her, to ever have been vulnerable enough to write song lyrics with a lover. "Really? You wrote lyrics?"

"Yup."

I am not convinced. "Really? You?"

Patricia crosses her arms in front of her chest. "Yes, really. Me. Is that so hard to believe?"

I do not answer, but just continue to look at her incredulously.

"*When the night rains, the moon will hold sway,*" she sings softly.

I can't help it—I clap in delight. "What? Was that one of the songs?"

Josephine smiles, and all at once I decide that I like her.

Patricia shakes her head.

"Is it? Is it?" I bounce up and down on the seat, playfully. "Sing more! Sing more."

A slight smile looks like it is spreading from the side of her mouth, something that happens only occasionally, as far as I can tell. "I can't. That's all I remember."

"Oh."

"He had a red sports car, and he taught me how to drive stick shift on it," she says. "I remember sitting there cross-legged on the floor at a friend's apartment when I told him I was pregnant with you. And the first thing he said is that we should get married. And my stomach was churning in knots because I knew I couldn't do it. I mean, I knew I could get out of a marriage if I had to, but I couldn't do that to a child."

"Do what to a child?" I feel so awake now. More awake than I can remember feeling in a very long time.

My mother, Patricia Powers, blinks. "Put a child in an unsafe situation."

I feel more confused than ever. "He was dangerous?"

"He . . . wasn't stable, Shannon," she says quietly. "He wouldn't have known how to be around a child."

I think back to the child I was at ten, when my birth father seemed to know enough about how to be around me. Even for such a short time. I think she has decided his story without really even trying to know him. Which I guess is fine for her, but she shouldn't be trying to encourage me to do the same.

"I see," I say, trying not to speak in anger. I am exhausted all over again, and I want this conversation to be over. "Weren't you going to show me some special ornaments on the tree or something?"

It is an inelegant transition, but both Patricia and Josephine accept it, and in another moment we are in the living room, looking at glass horses and handblown Santas from craft shows.

Connection

IN 2021, Facebook released an ad for a video calling device that featured a Black lesbian couple introducing their adopted daughter—who codes South Asian or perhaps Latina—to a pair of Black grandparents. It is a concise work of adoption genre fiction. The introduction takes place in front of a Christmas tree as the grandparents unwrap the device. One of the moms says the gift is "so you can get to know your new granddaughter." The grandmother looks over at the girl, hiding conspicuously behind her adoptive mom, and says, "We're so glad you're here." In the background, "Is This Love" by Corinne Bailey Rae plays.

Over the course of this thirty-second oeuvre, we see the shy young adoptee slowly come out of her shell, at first hiding behind her second adoptive mom when Grandma calls, then proudly showing her a progress report from school, and finally laughing with Grandma at an old school photo of her first adoptive mom while camped out under a beautiful tent made of a blanket with a colorful ethnic print. "Good night, Grandma," the girl says at the end of the call. The Grandma is quite moved by this, and asks, "Did you call me Grandma?" The girl just smiles.

Facebook calls this product "Portal."

Shannon Gibney is nineteen.

ON SUNDAY, which is the last day of my visit, we walk two houses over to Grandma Powers' house for dinner. Bobbi will pick me up in three hours, and we'll begin our drive back to Ann Arbor, getting in very late. But right now, stepping into my grandmother's modest foyer, I am simply looking for signs of Other Me. Of the portal. Anything will suffice: a stray curly hair, a pack of Lindt truffles on the counter. A dog-eared James Baldwin novel with a ripped piece of paper for a bookmark. Of course, the jackpot would be actually seeing her here, but after my brief discussion about it with Patricia and Josephine last night, that seems very unlikely. Is she really my grandmother's home health aide? How would that even have happened . . . and why? I have so many questions, but the way they are wrapping themselves tighter and tighter around my brain is making it hurt.

"Well, hello there!" Uncle Jim, Patricia's younger brother, says as we walk from the foyer into the living room. I am carrying a pan of freshly baked dinner rolls, and Patricia has a carafe of apple juice. Before I have a chance to set them down, Jim rushes me and envelops me in his arms. His grip is so tight I almost can't breathe. "I'm so glad you're here," he says when he releases me, and I see tears in his eyes. He is definitely the most expressive member of the family, and he and I sit down and talk about college, running, and Ann Arbor. He seems genuinely interested. Various family members interrupt at regular intervals, introducing themselves.

Patricia stands in a corner, talking to her sister Kathleen. Kathleen is a full-fledged nurse, not a nursing assistant like Patricia. Aunt Kathleen is still dressed in her scrubs from her morning shift. She looks tired. Patricia has told me that she works in the pediatric ward, which she says is much better on your body than the cardiac ward, where she is. *Nursing runs in the family,* she told me laughing, last night. The implication being that I would one day turn to the profession. So, there was an awkward silence when the laughing died out, and I didn't say anything.

We sit down at Grandma Powers' huge dinner table, where a pot roast, mashed potatoes, gravy, green beans, salad, rolls, and squash make a delicious-smelling spread. I am excited about everything except the squash.

I sit next to my cousin Paul, Aunt Bridget's son, who is in his early twenties, and across from Uncle Jim, who looks as ready to eat as I am.

"Bless us, O Lord, and these Thy gifts, which we are about to receive, from Thy bounty, through Christ, Our Lord. Amen," says Patricia, her voice hoarse and tired. I am relieved that it is the same prayer we say at my house in Ann Arbor.

I close my eyes during the grace, but for a minute as I open them, I think I see a young girl—maybe ten or so—seated beside Patricia. Her hands are clasped in prayer, her forehead bowed. Her curly hair is pulled back into two pigtails, and her skin is the same color as mine. The very same light brown with yellow undertones. When the prayer ends, she opens her eyes, and I swear for a minute that it's my eyes I'm looking at across the table. I blink, and my stomach drops in panic. *Where is the spiral?* When I blink again, she is gone.

"Erin?" Uncle Jim asks, across the table.

Everyone has begun serving themselves, passing the food around and taking portions. But they stop at the invocation of my birth name.

Uncle Jim realizes what he's done, with a start. "I mean, Shannon! Shannon. Sorry, I know who you are."

Shannon stares at him, confused for a moment. "Uncle Jim," she says slowly, coming back to herself.

"You just looked . . . spooked for a second. Are you okay, honey?" he asks, reaching for my hand across the table.

I pull it back quickly, resting it on my lap. "Fine," she says, smiling. "I'm fine." She still isn't sure what just happened, but she knows that sharing it with anyone at the table will only make things worse.

Uncle Jim lets out a short, uncomfortable laugh. "You sure?" he asks. "Because you don't look okay at all. You look like you've seen a ghost . . . Doesn't she look pale, Pat?"

Patricia is whispering something to Aunt Bridget. The two of them are giggling.

Uncle Jim sighs. The pot roast, mashed potatoes, and gravy are stopped with him, but he doesn't even care, he's so distracted. "Pat!" he says impatiently.

"What?" she asks crossly, before she catches herself. "What?" she asks again, in a nicer tone.

"Shannon," says Uncle Jim. "Doesn't she look pale to you?"

Patricia laughs, before she can stop herself. "Pale? Jimmy, what's gotten into you? She is the last person in the family anyone would describe as pale."

Everyone at the table, except for Grandma and Uncle Jim, laughs at that. Shannon doesn't think it's a funny joke at all, the fact that she is the only Black person at the table. In fact, Patricia saying so like that has created a growing hole in her stomach. And she thinks she can see a glimmering image of ten-year-old Other Shannon across the table, shaking her head at the comment, too.

"That's enough, Pat," Grandma Powers says softly.

Patricia gets a hold of herself, and everyone quiets down quickly.

Grandma Powers lifts a forkful of beef into her mouth, chews for a moment, then swallows. "The roast is delicious, isn't it?"

Everyone murmurs in agreement around the table. For a while, the only sound in the room is of silverware clinking, and glasses being lifted up and set back down. Shannon can focus on the succulent juice of the meat, the tangy bite of the salad dressing.

"Did anyone see all that construction going on over on Twelve, at Burrstone?" Aunt Bridget asks after a moment. She has Patricia's same dirty blond hair, the same rounded shoulders, thick with tension.

Aunt Kathleen groans. "God, that set me way back this morning. I was fifteen minutes late to my shift!"

Grandma Powers nods. "Yes, I think they plan to resurface that whole portion, all the way up to Five."

A collective groan follows, around the table.

"Of course that'll take them months to finish," says Uncle Jim.

"And when it's done, it won't be done right," says his girlfriend, Susan.

"It's never done right," says Aunt Kathleen.

"Because they don't know how to do it right, those people," says Patricia. "What they know how to do right is breed like rabbits."

I look up from cutting my meat, to see all of the grown-ups, including Uncle Jim, nodding in agreement.

"Mexicans damn near everywhere now," says Bridget.

My skin pricks. It feels translucent.

"Bridget," says Grandma Powers. "Don't swear at the dinner table."

Bridget smiles at Grandma Powers, across the room. "Sorry, Mom."

One year later, I will write this scene in a piece for an anthology of essays by children with queer parents to be produced by a small press. I will feel somewhat strange, submitting it, as I explain to the editor and in the essay itself that I have not actually grown up with my birth mother. But the editor will say that I express an important point of view, one that they otherwise don't have in the book. This essay will be my first published piece, so that when I receive page proofs two years after this dinner, I will think it important and appropriate to share them with Patricia. *She should know I am writing about her for a wider audience,* I will tell my boyfriend at the time. *She didn't ask me to write about her.* Later I will wish I had never shown her the essay, since she wouldn't have seen it otherwise. And it was a personal essay, after all, in which the writer is not bound by some kind of claim to objectivism, which you would find in journalism or scholarship.

It's all lies, Patricia will tell Shannon over the phone, while I weep and apologize. *I just don't understand why you would write something like this. Something so untrue. Are you really that mad at me? Do you really hate me this much? I wonder if you need therapy to resolve this, because telling lies is not the way to do it* . . . She will tell me that she will sue me if I publish the piece. She will say that our relationship is finished, and I will pull the essay from the collection, reasoning that she is more important to me than getting an essay published.

The problem is, of course, that our relationship is over anyway.

I have been trying to find a copy of the essay for twenty-five years, but it is lost to me in the hurricanes of paper I have moved to various residences in this time, now most likely living a second, third, or seventh life recycled as someone's term paper. I want to know what it was I said that had the force to remove my birth mother from me a second time. I want to read the words that bled her from the inside, the picture of her and her family so obtuse, so unbearably sharp.

But like her, they are gone to me now.

I was relinquished for adoption shortly after my birth,
by my white mother. She had had a brief and tumultuous
relationship with my African American birth father, and didn't
think that either of them could offer a baby a decent home.
I was nineteen when I found her again, after doing a birth
search. During the search, I also found out that my birth
father had died when I was six. Meeting my birth mother
after so many years, I was surprised to learn that she was
a lesbian. Her dalliances with men in her youth were her
attempt to deal with a sexuality that her working-class Irish
American family could not accept. So, I began to believe that
my birth mother's status as an "Other" in American society
would make her more able to connect with me as a mixed
Black woman—another "Other" in U.S. society. I could not
have been more wrong . . .

(These are the fractured bits of prose I can sift out of my consciousness so many years later. I can recall the thrust of the essay, its main
points, but not its style. Prose conveys the psychological texture of the
writer's mind as much as it reflects the substance of their speech, and
there is no way to alter my forty-eight-year old linguistic filter so that
it is twenty again.)

In 2019, more than twenty-five years after Shannon's reunion with
Patricia, and almost a decade after Erin's mother's death, one of Patricia's sisters will reply to a Facebook post about Shannon's experiences
at a children's literature conference in Stockholm with this comment:

I am happy for your success and accomplishments. Call it
WHITE but you are here because my sister loved you. She

wanted a better life for you than she could provide. Your parents did the same when they adopted you. Look past your skin color once. Delete this comment and me for that matter . . . who is racist really????? I won't say anymore though I truly could.

PART FOUR

More openings

WHEN THE BONDS OF KINSHIP ARE BROKEN AND REMADE, it shows you how porous and malleable they really are.

You are somebody's daughter because a child welfare law has decreed it.

Your family has forgone the idea and reality of blood and genetics (and race, for that matter) as *the* determining factors of ancestry and belonging.

In some very basic and important ways, you and your family are not *normal*. You do not perform kinship the way the majority of people and families you know and see in mainstream media do. For better and worse, your family formation is an aberration—which gets you thinking about other possible shapes your family could take. How relationships, like those between parent and child, seem immobile and permanent, but really are not. How things could easily be different, if a child was born in the generation ahead, the parent behind . . .

Shannon Gibney's parents are her children.

HE IS SURPRISED when a third portal opens up. The first two, of course, were to be expected, but this one? It is tilted and jagged and far more unstable than the other two. It cannot stay intact for more than a half hour at a time. Although that is certainly long enough to get an idea of where it leads, and what is happening on the other side. *Calculations lead to more calculations, which lead to new discoveries,* was what his father always told him, watching the endless papers and formulas spread across the dining room table proliferate, his namesake working till the wee hours of morning. Still, science, physics, should be more predictable than this. Or at least follow some discernible laws.

"Mom and Dad, calm down!" a young mixed Black woman says to two young white kids, running around a well-stocked kitchen. They are knocking over saltshakers and napkin holders and cups as they race each other.

The Black woman—the mother, apparently—looks so tired. And the more she pleads with them to settle down, the more boisterous they become.

"Sue, incoming!" says the little boy, throwing a cucumber long, into the dining room.

The blond girl with the deceivingly placid face pumps her arms and sprints. "I got it! I got it!"

"No!" Shannon yells. "Don't. You. Dare!"

And then it is like slow motion, when the girl, my mother who is not actually my mother at this moment, but inexplicably, beautifully, maddeningly, my child, leaps off the ground and actually gets some height, keeping her eyes on the fast-approaching cucumber my father has thrown her.

"You got it!" Jim yells.

Then Shannon screams, as Sue crashes into the lamp by the sliding glass doors, shattering the bulb instantly, and sending the stand straight into the wall. The girl lands easily on her stomach, the cucumber slipping through her hands.

Then the silence is deafening.

The mother's hands are covering her face like she doesn't want to look.

The little boy with the black hair is slowly inching his way toward the girl on the floor, who is now moaning softly. "Sue," *he is asking, a bit gingerly.* "You okay?"

The girl rolls over on her side and whispers, "Yes." *Several cuts from the glass run down her right arm. The jagged shards surround her.*

The mother can see that she plans to push herself up next, and that she will be cut by this, so she yells, "Stop!" *at the top of her lungs. For once, the children listen.*

I tiptoe carefully around the fallen plant, the salt and pepper everywhere across the floor. "Just wait. I'm coming." *She doesn't know why her children act like this. She doesn't understand what she needs to do to keep them safe. It is like there is something inside driving them, something they don't even comprehend.*

When she reaches the broken glass, she stops, about two feet away from her daughter. Then she gently shuffles the glass with her moccasin, collecting it in a small circle away from her.

By now, the girl has started crying in earnest.

"Just a minute," *Shannon says.* "I'm almost done."

The boy, hearing his beloved sister in pain, has actually started sniffling himself, on the other side of the room. He curls up on the futon, his big brown eyes trained on the whimpering lump thirty feet away.

The glass safely away, the mother lifts up her mother, and walks her past the now broken pieces of the dining room and kitchen. Why did I even have kids? *she wonders.* This was not what she signed up for. *And then, that thought leads to the next:* How did I even have kids? *She frowns.* It's so strange. They just appeared one day: BAM! Two little babies on her bed, and she's been running to keep up with them ever since.

"Let's get you cleaned up," she tells the girl, and kisses her on the forehead. Her daughter leans into her as they shuffle up the steps to the bathroom, the boy following them dejectedly, to clean and bandage the wound.

Erin Powers is twenty.

ERIN TAKES A LONG DRAG ON THE CIGARETTE, and then waits for the smoke to envelop her face. Not only does it warm her, but it makes her feel like she is in a movie, the protagonist covered in so much intrigue, you can't even make out her face. *An International Woman of Mystery.* Erin laughs, despite herself, and stomps the cold concrete. Winter in upstate New York is no fucking joke. Some things never change.

She is waiting outside the Greyhound station, her duffel bag filled with everything she's taking with her: two pairs of jeans, five pairs of underwear, two full sets of long underwear, two bras, four pairs of socks, three long-sleeved shirts, two short-sleeved shirts, half a stick of deodorant, a travel toothbrush and toothpaste, and three novels: *Beloved, Another Country,* and *The Woman Warrior.* She is trying to decide if she is going to use her last hundred dollars to buy a ticket . . . somewhere . . . or if she should just stay. Take Essie up on her offer to bunk at her place for a while, until she can get things sorted. Beg Bernie for her bartending job back. One thing is for certain: Something has to change. She cannot keep on like this.

Her cigarette is almost gone now, just ash, really. She sighs—it's her last one. She takes it from her mouth carefully, and then crushes it under her Doc Marten. Then she picks up her duffel and walks into the bus terminal. When she reaches the ticket counter, she tells the attendant that she wants a ticket to Detroit. A recent search through phone books she and Essie found in the library yielded several "Collins" listings in the area, her father's last name. Erin has always felt like if she could just *get there*, she could do some recon on her own, and maybe uncover something about him.

The thick white lady with a bad perm raises an eyebrow, probably thinking she's twelve, like everyone else. But she only says, "One way or round trip?" Erin pushes a wad of cash toward her and smiles ruefully. "Oh, one way," she says. "Definitely."

Shannon Gibney's children are her parents.

IF YOU WANT TO ENGAGE A WORMHOLE, you have to first identify or create it. No small feat. After that, you need a shitload of exotic matter, a magic ingredient which is basically repelled by gravity rather than expelled by it. Picture Professor Kohn, his appropriately eccentric physics instructor at Lawrence Tech all those years ago, lecturing to a full hall of half-listening undergrads: "The key to exotic matter lies in quantum fluctuations, which give empty space a kind of fizziness." He brushes off an imaginary piece of lint from his suit jacket, which only succeeds in striping it with the chalk he is frantically moving across the board. "Quantum theory says that subatomic particles and their attendant antiparticles are always moving in and out of existence in empty space. Exotic matter could come about by stopping this fizz, or as a physicist would say, by violating the ANEC—averaged null energy criteria . . ." Kohn smiles unexpectedly and catches his breath. Once he gets going like this, it's like an internal light is lit, and the energy just multiplies. Clearly, the man lives for science. And he imparts this love to his most dedicated students. "The notion of 'time loops' crisscrossing a wormhole, where sideways or backward time travel occurs (without its being able to alter the future), is also a theoretical possibility."

Picture a twenty-year-old Black male physics major, writing down these notes as fast as his hand can move the pencil across the paper. Picture his eyes alight with fascination, his every sense awake suddenly. *Maybe travel across the space-time continuum actually* is *possible. Maybe this shit is more than just a theory.* He grins to himself, all kinds of theorems, formulas, and computations beginning to pop in his mind. He is going to join the Air Force, but after that he is going to enroll at the University of Michigan and study particle physics with Professor Kohn's friend and colleague Dr. Lane, a world-renowned researcher in applied quantum theory. In fact, right at this moment, she is working on a super-secret method to gather copious amounts of exotic matter. The hope is that once all that gravitational energy is collected, it can be harnessed and directed toward punching open a door. A door to a wormhole.

He remembers all of this now, watching what he assumes is a second time loop pop out of the wormhole. A young girl who looks just like his daughter, Shannon, who visited him on that Palo Alto highway a few months before his death, sits on a couch between a twentysomething Black man who looks suspiciously like him but whom he cannot place, and a teenage Black girl who reminds him of his sister Delphine.

"But how do you know that I'm not a robot?" the girl asks her parents.

The girl's father sighs. "Because you have skin, and bones, and blood," he says. "Plus, you're breathing."

The girl frowns. "But they could have robots that could do that."

The girl's mother peers at her. "Do what?"

"Breathe. Like in Battlestar Galactica," *says the girl. She and her father watch the show religiously.*

"Shannon . . ." The girl's mother trails off.

"But I'm serious!" the girl exclaims, with the vehemence of an eight-year-old. "I could be a new prototype. Designed by someone in an alternate universe. Another timeline or something. Another dimension. And I could have a chip in my brain making me say and do everything I say and do. Making me think that I am the real *Shannon Gibney. When all along I am really just a* fake. *And you would never*

know it." *The girl frowns, then shifts in her seat uncomfortably. Now it appears that she is getting to what is* really *bothering her.* "I would never know it."

"Honey," *her father says, taking her hand.* "You know that you're here now, with me."

Shannon is looking off into the distance, at the woods behind their house. It is a place right beside home, but far enough away from it to be someplace else entirely. It is somewhere to go when you cannot really go anywhere. And there is a light inside it right now, faint, but growing under a low tree branch.

The girl's father reaches over to her and takes her chin in his hand, directing her eyes to his own. "Right?" *he asks.*

Shannon nods, clearly distracted. The words feel familiar somehow, even to him, like this has all been said before. "Yes," *she says.* "We're here. Now." *But where is* here? *she wonders. And when is* now?

"So we know at least that much is true, right?" *her father asks.*

The girl appears to try to focus on her mother and her words, but the light in the woods on the periphery of her sights is clearly calling her.

"This is all wrong," he says under his breath. "This is not how it should be."

Her father, Boisey the Third (or Fourth, depending on how you look at it), lets go of the girl's chin. "That's all we can know, sometimes. What's here and now. What could be, what could have been, what will be . . ."

Shannon's eyes follow the light contracting in the woods, and she grips the faded wood of her folding chair. "What's happening now, somewhere else . . . ," *she says.*

"All of that is just . . ." *Her dad waves his hands.* "Possibility."

"Possibilities," *she says, correcting her father.*

"Yes," her mother, Marwein, says. "Possibilities. We can never know without a doubt that you aren't an amazing bionic robot, and that there aren't multiple dimensions happening simultaneously, as you say . . ." There is a slightly rehearsed quality to her tone, as if she is saying this to say it, not because she knows or believes it.

The light is now gone, has diminished completely. But he and the girl have the sense that it will be back again, and soon. And that there is something there for them, in those woods. "Or that there aren't multiple me's living out their lives right now, on different timelines," she says.

Her mother, whose very curly hair is cut short into a dark brown halo around her head, squeezes her daughter's hand harder. "That could certainly be true," she says slowly, not really sure where the words are coming from. "It all depends on what you believe. And the little that we know, as human beings. And since we know that we're here now together, why worry about those infinite other possibilities? I know you're not a robot, my dear." Her mother laughs. "I'm sorry, I know you want to believe you're special . . . and you are . . . but not like that."

The girl laughs, too. They can't help it, these Collinses. Their minds sometimes get the best of them. She shakes her head. "No, I don't want to be a robot!"

Her father yanks playfully on one of her braids. "Good. 'Cause I don't want to raise a robot." He stands up. "Come on. Let's get a Popsicle."

PART FIVE

The Cancer Journals
(After Audre Lorde)

AUDRE LORDE was neither my birth mother nor my adoptive mother, but I consider her one of my essential creative mothers. And certainly, she is a spiritual mother. "Because I am woman, because I am Black, because I am lesbian, because I am myself—a Black woman warrior poet doing my work—come to ask you, are you doing yours?"

I stumbled upon her poetry and essays shortly after I began my complicated relationship with Patricia, in my early twenties. Lorde made me feel less alone and that the things the world was telling me were "wrong with me" perhaps had more to do with its oppressive structures than with me as an individual: "Each of us is here now because in one way or another we share a commitment to language, and to the reclaiming of that language which has been made to work against us." *Never a victim*, she insisted. Instead, become a relentless communicator of the way things are and of our responsibility to ourselves and each other.

Imagine my surprise when I discovered that we each received our breast cancer diagnosis in our early forties—her in 1977 and me in 2019. As writers do, she found refuge in her craft during her treatment and recovery, creating a series of raw essays and diary entries that later became the slim volume *The Cancer Journals*. This voice, this consciousness sent into the void, seemed to be speaking directly to me. To *me* . . . chronicling the unvarnished truths the female body will reveal by living through breast cancer: "The pain of separation from my breast was at least as sharp as the pain of separating from my mother. But I made it once before, so I know I can make it again."[2]

---

2.   "The Transformation of Silence into Language and Action." In *Sister Outsider: Essays and Speeches*, 40–44. Trumansburg, NY: Crossing Press, 1984. Lorde, Audre, and Adrienne Rich.

Holiday card from Patricia Powers.

Dear Sue, Jim, and Family,

I hope this year has been a happy, healthy, peaceful one for each and every one of you.

I continue to struggle with residuals of my fractured C-spine, resultant surgery and functional disabilities. I will be having more surgery later this month—minor.

Perhaps you do not know that approximately 8 months ago, my sister, Mary Sheila (I believe many of you have met her), was diagnosed with inflammatory breast cancer (IBC), an extremely aggressive, rare form of breast cancer. Her spirit and attitude have remained pretty much irrepressible, but it is and has been a tough fight. After chemo, Herceptin, surgery, and radiation, she now faces another course of chemo (axillary nodes positive). Please keep her in your thoughts and prayers as this will definitely be the definitive factor in her outcome. Shannon and Sue, I believe you two know her best. She was there when you were born Shannon . . .

I wish for all of you a peaceful Christmas filled with laughter and love.

My best wishes,
Patricia

Dear Sue, Jim, and Family,

I hope this year has been a happy, healthy, peaceful one for each and every one of you.

I continue to struggle with residuals of my fractured C-spine, resultant surgery and functional disabilities. I will be having more surgery later this month—minor.

Perhaps you do not know that approximately 8 mths. ago, my sister, Mary Sheila (I believe many of you have met her), was diagnosed with inflammatory breast cancer (IBC), an extremely aggressive, rare form of breast CA. Her spirit and attitude have remained pretty much irrepressible, but it is and has been a tough fight! After chemo, Herceptin, surgery, and radiation, she now faces another course of chemo (axillary nodes positive).

Please keep her in your thoughts and prayers as this will definitely be the definitive factor in her outcome. Shannon and Sue, I believe you two know her best. She was there when your were born Shannon. She and her husband will make a brief visit her during the holiday season.

Wishing you all the peace

and beauty

of the holiday season.

I wish for all of you a peaceful Christmas filled with laughter and love.

My best wishes,

Patricia

Excerpt from a letter Patricia Powers sent to Susan Gibney.

Sue,

I think at this time most especially, it would be appropriate to remind Shannon of her biological medical health history regarding breast cancer . . . I spent a lot of time during our communicative years stressing the importance of this to Shannon, but I am not certain she appreciates the importance of <u>diligent</u> breast health . . .

I have been evaluated genetically by the Feiner Institute and passed the info to Shannon. Unfortunately, there is still so much we don't know . . . The aggressive nature of Mary Sheila's cancer (Inflammatory Breast Cancer)—IBC—dictates an unfortunate risk for Shannon, that probably requires more than yearly mammo's (gamma mammo's), etc., etc.

So, I just felt the need to express the need for concern AGAIN, and know you are receptive to these concerns . . .

We Did It! 50,000 Women Strong...

-2-
See, -- I think this
time most espeeeally, it
would be appropriate to
remind Shannon of her
biological medical hx ie:
breast cancer... I spent
a lot of time during our
communicatiee — years stressy
the importance of this to
Shannon, but I am not
certain she appreciates the
importance of diligent breast
health with the medical hx....
I have been evaluated
senatiically by the Feiner
Institute →

THE
SISTER
STUDY
BREAST CANCER RESEARCH

we can make a difference!

1-877-4SISTER

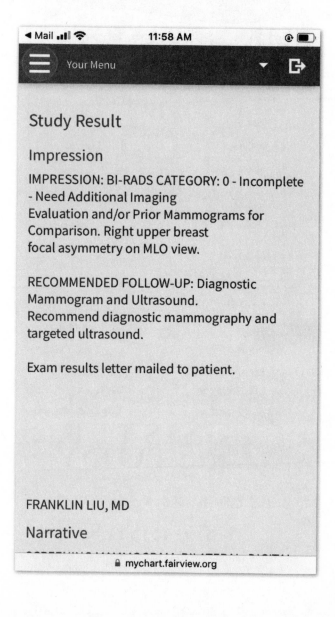

MINNEAPOLIS, MINNESOTA. OCTOBER 2019.

Shannon Gibney is forty-four.

◀ Mail ·ıll 🤶 11:58 AM ◉ 🔋

☰ Your Menu ▼ ➡

Study Result

Impression

IMPRESSION: BI-RADS CATEGORY: 0 - Incomplete - Need Additional Imaging
Evaluation and/or Prior Mammograms for Comparison. Right upper breast
focal asymmetry on MLO view.

RECOMMENDED FOLLOW-UP: Diagnostic Mammogram and Ultrasound.
Recommend diagnostic mammography and targeted ultrasound.

Exam results letter mailed to patient.

FRANKLIN LIU, MD

Narrative

🔒 mychart.fairview.org

Shannon Gibney
[redacted]
October 4, 2019
Date of Exam: 10/4/19

Dear Shannon Gibney:

Thank you for your recent visit.

Breast Imaging Result: Your recent breast imaging examination on 10/4/19 showed a finding that requires additional imaging evaluation. Most such findings are benign (not cancer). If you have already been called back for these tests, please disregard this letter. If not, please call 612-xxx-xxxx to schedule an appointment for these tests if you have not already done so.

Breast Density: Your mammogram shows that you have dense breast tissue. This means you have a slightly higher risk of getting breast cancer. It also means your mammograms will be harder to read, but it doesn't mean that mammograms aren't useful. In fact, yearly mammograms are even more important for women at higher risk.

Sincerely,
Interpreting Radiologist

Dear Shannon,

I would like to extend my support to you during this difficult time as you learn more about your new diagnosis of breast cancer.

Enclosed are educational materials and resources others have found helpful.

I am the Nurse Coordinator in breast care at Fairview Southdale Breast Center with many years of oncology and surgical experience. I am able to answer questions about the diagnosis, treatment options, assist with appointment scheduling, and offer support resources as you move through planning and treatment.

Please do not hesitate to contact me for assistance.

I look forward to talking with you.

Sincerely,
Breast Nurse Coordinator
Fairview Southdale Breast Center

Dear Shannon,

I would like to extend my support to you during this difficult time as you learn more about your new diagnosis of breast cancer.
Enclosed are educational materials and resources others have found helpful.

I am the Nurse Coordinator in breast care at Fairview Southdale Breast Center with many years of oncology and surgical experience. I am able to answer questions about the diagnosis, treatment options, assist with appointment scheduling, and offer support resources as you move through planning and treatment.

Please do not hesitate to contact me for assistance.

I look forward to talking with you.

Sincerely,

Breast Nurse Coordinator
Fairview Southdale Breast Center

Telephone

Gibney, Shannon

DOB: 1/30/1975

— most common type 80% of breast cancers — more predictable

Diagnosis: *Invasive Ductal Carcinoma*

Clinical Stage I

Size: *1.0cm — very small*

Receptors:

Estrogen(ER)- ⊕ } *positive*
Progesterone(PR)- ⊕

HER-2/neu- ⊖ *negative*

grade 1 : low grade, less aggressive
grade is what cells look like under microscope

Types of treatment for breast cancers:
1. Surgery *— First Step*
   a. Lumpectomy vs Mastectomy, sentinel lymph node biopsy.
2. Radiation Therapy
   a. Directed by Radiation Oncologist.
3. Chemotherapy
   a. Directed by Medical Oncologist.
4. Hormone Therapy-Tamoxifen, Aromatase Inhibitors
   a. Directed by Medical Oncologist for hormone receptor positive breast cancer.
5. ~~Targeted Therapy~~ *— You are not a candidate for this.*
   a. ~~Directed by Medical Oncologist for Her-2/neu positive breast cancer.~~ *Her 2 ⊖.*

1. Surgery: *— Same Day Surgery*
   a. Lumpectomy followed by radiation: *— Sentinel node will be tested also.*
      i. Lumpectomy-removes the cancer along with a small rim of normal healthy tissue (negative/clean margin).
      ii. Goal of a lumpectomy is to remove the cancer while keeping as much of the breast as possible.

   3-5% risk of recurrance

      iii. You will need to come to the breast center the day of the procedure for Seed Localization.
         1. Seed localization-marker is placed, by radiologist, at original biopsy site. This seed allows the surgeon to locate the cancer during the surgery. The cancer, seed, and normal tissue are all removed.

   equal survival rate 20 years out

      iv. Outpatient procedure-will go home the same day.
      v. Risks/Complications-excessive bruising or bleeding, infection, fluid collection (seroma), numbness or loss of sensation, change in breast shape.
      vi. Recovery-increase your activity gradually.
      vii. Radiation is recommended after a lumpectomy.
         1. This will be discussed in greater detail by radiation oncologist. Consult will be arranged after post-op visit with surgeon.
         2. Radiation is given to decrease the risk of recurrence at tumor bed site.

   b. Mastectomy: *— 1-2 nights in hospital*

   1-2% of risk of recurrance

      i. During a mastectomy, the surgeon removes all of the breast tissue, plus the nipple and areola. *⊕ Sentinel lymph node biopsy*
      ii. You may choose to have breast reconstruction.
         1. You will meet with a plastic surgeon to discuss reconstruction options in greater detail.
      iii. Inpatient stay-1-2 nights.
      iv. Drains will be placed at time of surgery and you will go home with drains in place.

✱ Oncotype: If score >25-chemo would be recommended
This is a test that may be ordered after your surgery, that tells us if chemotherapy would be recommended, because your risk of recurrance is higher.

Nurse coordinator's notes on Shannon Gibney's diagnosis.

    v. These drains will stay in place 1-2 weeks following the surgery. The drains help remove fluid that collects following the surgery.

    vi. Risks/Complications-pain or numbness, bleeding or infection, stiffness of the shoulder, fluid collection (seroma), long term swelling of the arm (lymphedema), wound healing problems.

    vii. Recovery-3 to 6 weeks for optimal recovery.

  c. Sentinel Lymph Node Biopsy-
    i. Removal of the first 1-3 lymph nodes that drain the breast.
      1. If proceeding with a lumpectomy-final pathology from sentinel lymph node biopsy will be back in 2-3 days.
      2. If proceeding with a mastectomy-lymph nodes removed will be sent to pathology at time of surgery for a frozen diagnosis. If positive-proceed with axillary lymph node dissection.

2. Radiation therapy-
  a. Discussed in greater detail with radiation oncologist.
  b. Starts 4-6 weeks after surgery.
  c. It is daily (Mon-Fri) for approximately 4-6 weeks.
  d. Common side effects:
    i. Fatigue
    ii. Sunburn like appearance
    iii. Possible blistering or peeling

3. Chemotherapy-
  a. Discussed in greater detail with medical oncologist.
  b. Chemotherapy can be given before surgery and/or after surgery.

4. Hormone Therapy – *An Oncologist will prescribe this for you after Surgery.*
  a. Discussed in greater detail by medical oncologist for ER/PR positive disease.

5. ~~Targeted Therapy~~
  a. ~~Discussed in greater detail be medical oncologist for Her-2/neu positive disease.~~

The Plan:
- Schedule Surgery — Beth.
- Genetics —
- you will need a pre-op physical with your primary provider.

- you will need a good Supportive sports bra or 2 to wear 2 weeks following Surgery. front closure, no underwire.

- results from surgery will be back 2-3 days after Surgery & Dr. Schulte will call you to inform.

Nurse coordinator's notes on Shannon Gibney's diagnosis, continued.

THE TRUTH IS, I OFTEN THINK OF MY TUMOR. When the doctor cut it out, what did it look like? Did he or the nurses even look at it? Or was it just another cancerous mass that needed little observation, besides its subsequent evaluation by laboratory scientists under the microscope? Surgical teams remove so many tumors, they must become banal after a time. A routine overgrowth of cells that needs to be stopped before it spreads and takes over the whole system.

For some reason, whenever I imagine my tumor, it is white. Round with scalloped edges. I have no idea if this is true, and no real interest in verifying its accuracy. It is only what I imagine.

Sometimes I wish I had asked the doctor if I could have kept the tumor. In a jar or something. It was a part of me, no matter how errant, and now that it has been removed, I would like to observe it. This thing I had no idea was inside me, growing, multiplying, plotting my demise. This thing, it seems, is part of what was passed down to me from my birth mother. Or at least, her family. I would like to attempt to decipher the story of the cells in this. What do they have to say? Were they waiting for the right environmental trigger, or would they have appeared anywhere at any time, the DNA preprogrammed from my grandmother's body to my mother's to mine?

And of course, the body remembers all that is lost. Even those parts that were trying to kill it. Eventually. Even the cancer I was lucky they found on a routine mammogram, early, before it had time to spread and infect other organs and systems. I was lucky, yes, I was vigilant. Because unlike most adoptees, I knew something of this story of the family body, passed down for generations. I was *warned*. And I am thankful to still be here, to be able to raise my kids. To write these words.

Late at night and at random times during the day, I will feel a sharp pain on the right side of my chest (the nurse told me they are so common among breast cancer survivors; they call them *zingers*), as my body recalls that something was cut from me. Something was excised. It might have been small, a centimeter and a half in diameter, and it might have been new and deadly, but it was there, and it left its mark. Even now, seven months after surgery, my underarm, where they took samples of the lymph nodes to make sure the cancer hadn't spread, is still numb from halfway down. The doctor told me this will last for some time, but will slowly dissipate. Indeed, little slivers of feeling will return week by week, month by month. The skin of my right breast and right upper chest, though no longer raw and red and peeling, is still darker, after so much radiation was shot at the tumor site, to kill any remaining cancer cells that may not have been cut out during surgery. There is a small node at the tumor site—hard and round. It is an evolving group of blood cells attempting to heal themselves after being severed during surgery. I believe my oncologist called it a *hematoma*. It is the strangest sensation to feel an itch *inside* your skin—but that is exactly the sensation the hematoma elicits. Like a scab repairing itself that you just can't reach.

The body remembers.

And has its own story to tell.

Prediction

EVEN A CANCEROUS FAMILY TREE is a family tree for an adoptee. And therefore, to be cherished . . . if also maligned. This genetic map I received after my treatment is probably the fullest, and certainly the most professional, genealogical rendering of either side of my immediate biological family I will ever receive. In that sense, the fact that it contains information on BRCA1 and BRCA2 genes, pathogenetic mutations, and unknown variants is immaterial. An adoptee will take any breadcrumbs, even carcinogenic ones.

And yet, with genetics as with all things, there is still so much we don't know. I tested negative for all known high-risk genes that cause breast cancer. Which means that I did not pass them on to my son or daughter, although they will have to be diligent about preventative screening. I wept when my genetic counselor told me this news, which she assured me was "very, very good." In this vein, I thought it might be more appropriate to call my particular genetic map of cancer *A Non-Cancerous Family Tree.*

Although I am genuinely a failure at reading maps, even the geographically illiterate can take a look at my genetic map and see that something is going on with the Powers women, with their high rates of cancer (especially breast). For all her warnings and worry of breast cancer, Patricia ended up dying of an extremely rare and deadly cancer called anaplastic carcinoma. According to my aunt Bridget, it "spread to intestines, pancreas, uterus/ovaries—couldn't be exact as it was found and she passed within days. It was very aggressive and unknown as to where it started." Almost 40 percent of adults will get cancer at some point in their lives, so maybe this is not so surprising after all? Everyone has someone in their family who has survived or perished from it. But certainly, where there are clusters of it within families and through generations, questions will be asked, concerns piqued that it cannot simply be a coincidence. There are many small genes they haven't mapped yet. And others that can get triggered by environmental factors. And of course, the complex interplay between multiple genes, and genes and the environment, is now widely accepted as the cause of cancers. Something so elusive that it can be virtually impossible to pinpoint, much less map.

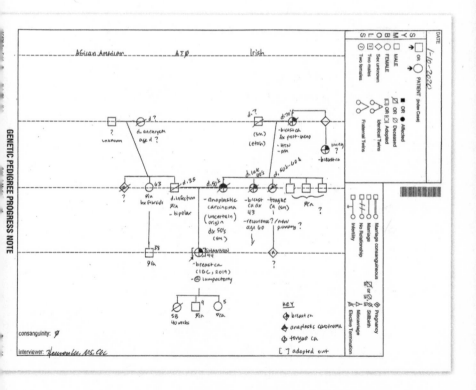

Shannon Gibney's genetic family tree.

PART SIX

Everything comes back

Aunt Annette, Boisey Collins Jr., and Uncle Boisey Christopher Collins,
in Detroit, date unknown.

Excerpt from a phone call.

BOISEY CHRISTOPHER COLLINS (or the bridge between grandfather, father, uncle, daughter and grandson): *I was adopted by my stepmom, Yvonne Collins, when my father, Boisey Collins Sr., married her. There is no other man on earth I respected as much. He had his flaws, but he was the most kind and compassionate person I have ever known. Everyone in the neighborhood would just call him "Pops." He was a jack-of-all-trades, man. He could fix anything! He used to have all the neighborhood kids over at the house. He would give them jobs. Everyone loved him. That's why, when I was eleven and they were legalizing the adoption, I said that I wanted to be named after my stepdad (I call him my dad, Boisey Collins). So from then on, my legal name was "Boisey Christopher Collins."*

Everyone tried to talk me out of it, but I wouldn't budge.

No one on that side of the family (Collins) will call me that, though. I understand why . . . They all call me "Christopher," but everyone else in my life I met afterward knows me as "Boisey."

I was just talking on how the whole "y" on Boisey is like a mystery. In our family, everyone spells it "Boisey," and the common spelling is just with an "e." The French spelling. People in the family told me years ago that during that time in Hattiesburg, Mississippi, in the 1920s, '30s, and '40s, it was a very common name. And there was a strong French culture in Mississippi in that time period—not just in Louisiana—that stretched all the way to Florida. With French culture and influence, there was actually a lot of people named Boisey, with the "y" on the end. Only thing I could think of is that it's a Black cultural thing—it's similar to how Black people put a twist on different names, and add their own spelling to it. Because I haven't really found a reason for it, other than that. So, it's pretty cool that it is a tradition that looks like it might have stretched all the way back to the turn of the century. That Black culture having a different way of spelling and naming, and whatnot.

From what I hear in France, it's still a common name. I kind of would like to do a little research from the French side of it, to see how common it really is over there. It means "forest," or "green, quiet forest."

Everyone in the family just called your father "Junior," since he was "Boisey Collins Jr." I don't have that many memories of spending time with him, because he was twenty-five years older than me. But I do remember playing guitar and smoking weed with him down in the basement. He could play that guitar, boy.

Did anyone talk to you yet about your father's mental health? I don't want to shock you if you didn't already know that he was bipolar. He dodged the draft for Vietnam; that was why they kicked him out of the Air Force.

Everyone, whenever they mentioned your father, would always talk about how brilliant he was. How charming, how good-looking. But I just had the feeling that he never really had the chance, the resources, to really develop those things for himself. And your grandfather, my father, was the same way. Do you know he was the first Black electrician at the Mound Road Engine Chrysler Plant, in 1954? But I always felt he should have been doing so much more than that—I mean, he was brilliant! The most brilliant man I ever met.

Erin Powers is twenty.

HE IS A YOUNG MAN, maybe around the same age as I am, with a wide chest and a muscular frame. Come to think of it, he kind of looks like one of those bodybuilders on TV that Aunt Bridget's boyfriend is always watching. His legs look like long tree trunks, anchored into the ground. When we sit down at the table, I think that he'll maybe topple it over, his upper half is so big. But he doesn't. He just slides in there, with like a half inch between him and the table's edge. Somehow, he makes it look easy, relaxed, like he could fit in wherever he goes as long as he tries. But then, once you take a look at his eyes, you realize that that's what he's probably been doing his whole life—trying to fit in here and there, with this family or that family . . . Because there is a sadness to them. An intelligence, also, but definitely a weight.

"That's quite a story," I say, moving my pen across the paper as fast as I can. This is the first real break I have had on any significant information on my father's side of the family, and I do not want to miss even a preposition. "A name passed down for three, maybe four generations like that. And you deciding to take it up, as a child."

He takes a sip of the ice water he has ordered. "Yeah. Sometimes you get something in your head that no one else can understand. A notion, I guess. And nothing and no one can talk you out of it."

I laugh. "I know a little about that."

He smiles for the first time since we sat down at the cafe. It is an open and generous smile, but again, a bit sad. "Yep, I suppose you would."

He is pretty impressed with me, coming all the way from Utica on my own, not even bothering to get my bearings or check into a motel before heading over to the nearest Wayne County library, and thumbing through the area phone books until I found the two entries under "Boisey Collins." The one piece of information Essie and I were able to find in all our searching: the name of my father. Which even my mother kept under lock and key. Or maybe she convinced herself she forgot it? Or maybe she actually did . . . ? When I think of her, my windpipe constricts. I see her in the hospital, hooked up to too many tubes, barely breathing. When the time came, I could not bring myself to enter the room to say good-bye. I'm still not sure why, although I have plenty of theories.

"It's just really a blessing you found us at all, with all these years and miles and deeds gone by," he says. "I just really wish you had called this time last year. Because the other Boisey Collins in that phone book was your grandfather, Boisey Collins Sr. He died last June."

I frown, feel a flutter in my chest.

The server shows up and asks us if we want anything, and I wave her away absently, saying that we need more time.

"I'm so sorry," I say. Then I think I might sound disingenuous, or unclear or something. I shake my head. "I'm so sorry about your father." I feel my face color. *This is so confusing. Is he Boisey Collins III? Or Two and a Half, if that side of the family won't acknowledge his name?* "I mean, my grandfather."

Boisey Christopher is looking at me strangely. I wonder if he feels as split by his story as I do. I take a deep breath.

"But what about my father?" I press on. I still can't really believe my uncle is in front of me now, and that due to the odd laws of adoption and family relations, he is just about my age. He's filling in so many of the blanks I've tripped over my entire life, which Mom tried to convince me weren't there at all, even as I was in the middle of tripping.

Then Mom's voice in my ear, whispering something she told me a long time ago: *He . . . wasn't stable, Erin. He wouldn't have known how to be around a child.* I wave the voice away from my ear, like you would a fly.

Boisey Christopher raises an eyebrow. "I told you everything I know about him. I'm sorry I don't have more stories. Like I said, he was so much older than me that we weren't even really in the house together that much."

I place my hands in my lap under the table, and make one hold the other, so he won't see them shaking. "But the way you talked about him . . . it was in the past tense. Like he was dead or something. But he's not, right?"

The look he gives me is downright fearful, so then I just blurt out, "He's not dead . . . ?"

Boisey Christopher sighs deeply. He sits up straight in his chair. "No, he's not dead."

But something about the way he says it makes me wary. Still, I breathe out a sigh of relief.

He calls over the server and orders a burger with everything on it, and asks if I want anything. I shake my head vigorously. I'll be lucky if I can eat at all on this trip, with all the excitement.

He sets the menu down beside him, and then meets my eyes. I can't help but notice that his are a little wet around the edges, which produces a pang in my gut. "Look, Erin," he says, and my name sounds good and open—*recognizable.* "Your father's not dead, but he's been missing for a good fourteen years now. Disappeared on December 20, 1981."

I am aware that I am holding my breath.

He continues. "Working at this place he called his lab, although near as anyone could tell, it was just a junkyard. A collection of bits and parts of engines and tanks and generators he collected for years, and stored there." Boisey Christopher pauses, and then takes another sip of water.

Under the table, my right hand is smushing the left.

"I mean, I was just a kid when all this was going down, so I didn't understand . . . I just absorbed bits and pieces of the story from the adults around me, you know? So, just keep in mind that I don't know how much of this is really the truth . . ." He rubs the back of his neck. "But everyone said he was just nuts right before he . . . um . . . disappeared. Talking about building some kind of machine. Working all hours of the day and night, running calculations about this time loop or that one. Your aunt Annette said he wouldn't shut up to her about something like—what was it called? Exotic matter? Something crazy. He would go off his meds sometimes . . . and they weren't even that good back then, anyway, when he *was* on them."

The server comes, and sets his plate in front of him. I can see that he is relieved to have a brief break in the conversation.

I feel more awake right now than I have ever felt in my entire life. *Did he build the wormhole?* I rub my forehead. I don't think I'm thinking straight, right at the one moment when it would be most useful to do so. *No, he wouldn't have* built *it. More like created something to open a doorway to it. Maybe even figured out how to use it to travel to different locations in the space-time continuum?* I am busy accessing every *Star Trek* episode I ever watched, every book on wormholes and Einstein's theory of general relativity I checked out from the library. *If he went missing, maybe he got trapped inside it somehow?* My stomach flips. *He could be on another timeline! Maybe even with the girl who looks like me. Or he could be in some in-between region, some space below or above what we can see from our particular location in this universe.* I laugh, despite myself. *My long-lost and much-maligned father, existing on the edge of a black hole, harnessing its power interdimensionally . . . What if?*

Thankfully, Boisey Christopher has been completely absorbed in his burger this whole time, and I don't think he has picked up on all the insane calculations I have been making while he eats his lunch.

I shift in my seat, suddenly conscious that I am getting overheated in all my snow gear from New York. It is warmer here, and there is almost no snow. I begin peeling off my jacket, and throw my hat to the ground. Then I write down as much as I can, every single word I can remember just as he said it. It feels like someone has let a long-pent-up dam loose inside me, and the water is finally rushing free. After a few minutes, I set down my pen and massage my hand. I have forced it to write too much, too fast, and it hurts. But I don't care. I have the sense that I should be careful with what I want to ask next—that it could either end the conversation, or scare my newfound, unlikely uncle. But I have never known how to proceed in any direction but forward, for good and for bad. "Where is this place? That lab you mentioned? Can you take me there?"

Boisey Christopher carefully wipes his mouth with his napkin, his burger all but dust on his plate. He looks at me, tired and still sad. "Look, I get it. It's your dad, who you been looking for most of your life, it sounds like . . . But that was fourteen years ago, Erin. And fourteen years ain't nothing."

I lean back in my seat, fold my arms across my chest.

This makes him sit up straighter in his own chair. "The police did a thorough job, I can tell you that. Went back numerous times and conducted a lengthy investigation. Never found anything." He leans forward. "Not a thing."

I can't help the frown spreading across my face.

"So you have to ask, if trained professionals couldn't find anything, why do you think you'd suddenly have more luck after all this time?" He's not saying it in a mean way at all. His tone is just matter-of-fact. Which makes me angrier, for some reason.

"Because I'm his daughter," I say quietly. I am a bit shocked, because I didn't know I was going to say that.

Across the table, Boisey Christopher looks uncomfortable. "The daughter who never met him," he says. Then he reaches across the table to take my hand, unexpectedly. "Look, I'm not trying to be cruel here. I'm just trying to be real."

"Look . . ." I think of Mom, loving me her whole life, me loving her, each of us desperately trying to understand the other, and failing just as desperately. "Can you just take me there?" I hope my voice doesn't sound as frantic as I feel.

He sighs deeply, looks out the window at the vast parking lot, mostly empty of cars. And that is the moment I know he will take me.

Shannon Gibney is forty-four.

EVEN THOUGH I HAVEN'T EATEN ANYTHING YET this morning, I feel strangely full, all of Boisey Christopher's words piling up in my stomach. I am sitting in the middle of a grassy field, scribbling in a journal as fast as I can. If I miss something—anything—it is a detail I fear I may never retrieve again about my father, my uncle, and the Collins family.

"But your son," he says. "You named him Boisey, too?"

"Yep. With a 'y' at the end," I say, smiling.

He clears his throat on the other end. "That almost brought me to tears when I read that yesterday."

He is referring to the brief chat we had on Facebook Messenger. I found him there, after twenty years, and reached out hoping to fill in some of the blanks I have about that side of the family for this book I am writing. And for myself, and my children.

"My son is amazing," I tell him. "I'm biased, of course, but I think he lives up to the legacy of the name. Hopefully, you'll have the chance to meet him soon, when we head back home for the holidays. He will be very excited to hear all this history about his name."

Boisey Christopher clears his throat again, and I wonder if that is how he pushes down his wounds. "So, tell me about this book you're writing," he says, changing the subject.

I laugh uncomfortably. I am staying in a giant old mansion in Red Wing for two weeks, on retreat with five other women artists, ostensibly to get work done on my book. "It's . . . weird," I tell him. "Like, really weird." I pull out a blade of grass and stare at it. I admire its abiding greenness. "It's about stories, and ruptures, and family. Worm-holes and timelines where your life looks completely different . . . where *you* actually are different because of choices maybe your parent made." I scratch my head, regretting dragging him into this particular rabbit hole. The truth is, I don't even know what the hell I'm doing. That's probably why I'm still interested. "I don't know. I have trouble describing it."

There is a long pause, and I watch an old Trans Am inch its way around the curvy edge of the field I am sitting in. I am just about ready to admit defeat and say good-bye, when his quiet yet sturdy voice comes through. "You know, it's amazing how many things I still don't know myself, about my family history. How much stuff just gets swept up under the rug."

And that's when I realize that if I've been botched by my story—by the possibilities that were lived, imagined, and never even conceived of—he surely has been, too. At the very least, we are both adoptees who felt that fracture from childhood.

"What about your birth mother?" he asks.

I feel my body stiffen. It has been five years since her death, and at least ten since we spoke to each other. There is nothing I regret, but so many things that I wish could have been different. "What about her?" I ask, my voice small.

"I mean . . . I hope it's not too personal to ask, but why did she give you up for adoption? I heard things in the family about Junior hav-ing another child that was given away for adoption, but I never really knew."

Now it's time for me to clear my throat. Out come the words I have said so many other times, to so many other people. "She just didn't think she or my father could give me the kind of life I needed or de-served. She was an alcoholic, and it sounds like he wasn't stable . . . So, all things being equal, she was probably right."

The thing about words is, they give the illusion of finality. Like once you say how something is, for all intents and purposes that's how it *is*. Or how it was. Which is one of the reasons why I hate the words to this particular story. Because there is so much those words erase. So many possibilities and realities that I don't even know. But at least I know that I don't know. To anyone hearing the story, the words define absolute reality.

"Okay," says Boisey Christopher. "I get it."

And if anyone actually *could* get it, it would be him.

Somewhere in time and space, Boisey Collins Sr. is tucking Boisey Collins Jr. into bed. Neither has any idea that I am coming, that Boisey Christopher is already on his way to them, and that after they are gone my son will complete the circle.

"You know, I really wish I could have met him," I say. The memory of my father's shocked expression on the other side of the portal, seeing me when I was ten, floods my vision. I shake it off. "I mean, *your* father. I really wish I had actually met him . . . It was good to talk to him on the phone, but—"

"Yeah, in person is just different." Boisey Christopher finishes my thought.

"It is," I say. "It really is."

```
                  To smile in autumn
921
Parks          Parks, Gordon, 1912-
                  To smile in autumn : a memoir /
               Gordon Parks. -- 1st ed. -- New York :
               Norton, c1979.
                  249 p. : ill. ; 25 cm.
```

Boisey Collins   313-

Detroit, MI 48234

```
                  1. Afro-American photographers--
               United States--Biography.  I. Title

MiAa    16 JAN 80      5285967   EY HAdc       79-19225
```

Library card catalog card with Boisey Collins Sr.'s address.

Shannon Gibney is twenty.

SHANNON STARES AT THE LIBRARY INFORMATION CARD she has
stolen from the card catalog at the Wayne County Public Library. She
has never stolen anything in her life before, so it felt odd to rip it from
the drawer when she thought no one was watching, and surreptitiously
copy the information she found for the one phone-book entry under
"Boisey Collins." But she needed it. She and Bobbi drove to this strange
library in suburban Detroit with the express purpose of thumbing
through the appropriate phone book to find her grandfather. And once
she found him, she realized they had brought no paper. Thus the Gordon Parks entry ripped from the card catalog. Thus, her lipstick stain as
she pressed the card anxiously after copying everything down. *Could
it really be this easy?*

And now they are back home in Bobbi's room. Sitting on the edge
of her bed. Crammed together, staring at the cordless phone, contem-
plating dialing the numbers.

"And what the hell did I think I was going to do now?" I ask her. I
absently itch a mosquito bite on my arm. Outside, we can hear the girls
next door playing hopscotch and double Dutch on the sidewalk.

Bobbi shrugs. "I'm not saying it's not weird, calling a relative you've
never met out of the blue. But you've done it before."

Patricia. She is talking about meeting Patricia last December. And
our relationship that has progressed since then, with more phone calls
and letters. This is what I wanted. So many stories that I never knew

I needed have come to me through her. But I am also beginning to see that my new connection with my birth mother is just another complex relationship to negotiate.

Bobbi holds the library information card between her index and middle fingers, tapping it on my knee. A medium-sized fan sits in her window in front of us, blowing out hot July afternoon air. I sometimes think about what it would have been like to do any of this on my own. And my mind goes blank. She is always there, answering the phone in the early morning, helping to plan another trip to a strange place we know nothing about, piecing together incomplete documentation, brainstorming plans A, B, and C.

I snatch the card from her fingers and then begin dialing. We already know that the other Boisey Collins, my father, is dead. We found the death certificate last summer. Date of death: December 20, 1981. Died from injuries sustained in a high-speed police chase in Palo Alto, California. Buried out there, in Santa Clara County. And right now, *his* father may be the only link I have to him, and that side of the family. The phone begins to ring. I tap my knee, feeling a spot of hair around the top that I missed while shaving this morning.

"Hello?" It is unmistakably the voice of an older man.

"Um, hello," I say. My voice even sounds shaky to my own ears. "This is . . . Shannon Gibney. Your granddaughter."

Bobbi locks her arm in mine, leans her head on my shoulder.

I exhale.

"My granddaughter?" He sounds surprised, but actually not *that* surprised. And then he says, "You Junior's daughter?" which just sucks my breath away. *Did he already know? Was I an open secret?*

"Yes," I say in a small voice. The sound of the whirling fan gets louder in the cramped room. I see my father, his perplexed face and shaking hands, all those years ago on the side of that highway in Palo

Alto. And I wonder how this man, my grandfather, would react if I told him about the portal, and the moment I met his son.

"You know, we always wondered if there was a child of his out there somewhere," he says. "Actually, suspected as much."

"Really?" I can't help it—I laugh. *Was my father a rolling stone? Am I just one in a brood of his children?*

And then my grandfather laughs, too. "Yeah. I mean . . . Junior was . . . complicated."

"Okay," I say. I consider the possibility that my father might have told him, or anyone, about our interdimensional meeting. He could have. But more likely, he decided to keep it to himself, for fear of being even more misunderstood by loved ones than it sounds like he already was.

My grandfather interrupts my musings. "You know he passed, right?"

I nod.

Bobbi elbows me in the ribs.

"I mean, yes!" I glare at her. "I know. We found that out last year. That he died when I was six."

"Um-hmm," he says.

The sound of kids' delighted screaming punctuates the otherwise quiet of the afternoon. I stand up and peer through the fan, out the window. The neighborhood kids have abandoned hopscotch, and are now engaged in a lively water fight.

"I live in Ann Arbor," I say, again because it seems like I should say something. "And also, Pittsburgh. I mean, I go to college in Pittsburgh."

The old man, who is my grandfather, laughs. "Ann Arbor, huh? That's not far from us at all. Just think of it: All this time, you were just over here, down the road."

"All this time," I say, thinking about my cousins, who live across town and who we saw every other weekend growing up. Would it have been like that, knowing that my grandfather and the Collins family were just a little farther away?

We will get off the phone a few minutes later, promising to call each other again, which we will, and also to meet each other in person, which we won't. It's not that we don't want to actually interact, but that we both have family, school, and work obligations. And also, that the whole premise of the storyline, what we are to each other, what we could have been, is so awkward. My grandfather will tell me that I have a living uncle, also named Boisey, around my same age. He will give me this uncle's email address and I will write him when I get back to college. We will continue this correspondence for a couple of years, and then drop off.

Shannon Gibney is twenty-three.

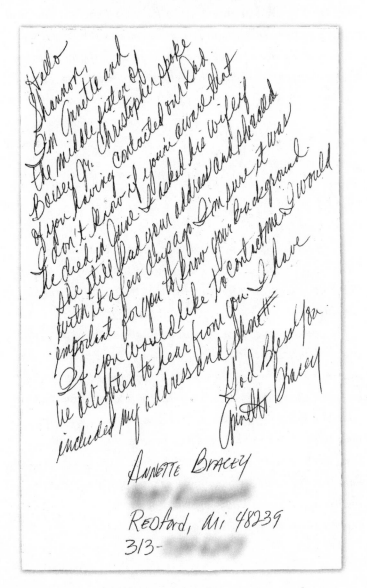

Hello Shannon,

I'm Annette and the middle sister of Boisey Jr., Christopher spoke of you having contacted our Dad. If you're aware that he died in June I asked his wife if she still had your address and she would. I don't know if you're aware that with it a few days ago. I'm sure it was important for you to know your background. Of you would like to contact me, I would be delighted to hear from you. I have included my address and phone.

God Bless You

Annette Bracey

ANNETTE BRACEY

Redford, Mi 48239

313-

Hello Shannon,

I'm Annette and the middle sister of Boisey Jr. Christopher spoke of you having contacted our Dad. I don't know if you're aware that he died in June. I asked his wife if she still had your address and she called with it a few days ago. I'm sure it was important for you to know your background. If you would like to contact me, I would be delighted to hear from you.

God Bless You,
Annette Bracey

June 12, 1998
Dear Shannon,

I was glad when I received your letter your mother was kind enough to write upon receiving my letter to you. Please thank her for me. I hope your trip was successful. It sounds exciting!

It would be nice to meet you and have a long talk. Family situations are difficult at the best of times but I'm sure it was frustrating when you didn't know about your background. It must of taken courage and determination to go about finding your biological father. I know you don't know a lot about your father but I can tell you this, he was a very complex person. He was very intelligent and often we didn't understand him, but I'm sure he gave you some part of his intelligence. Just from the little I know of you. I hope we can meet when you come for your visit . . . Sincerely,

Annette Bracey

Annette Bracey and Shannon Gibney, in 1998.

Shannon Gibney is forty-four.

WE ARE SITTING IN MY AUNT ANNETTE'S LIVING ROOM, on her leather sofa. I am sipping ice water, and the kids are in the kitchen with their juice. I can hear Annette asking them if they want a little more, and I smile at the way Aunties always spoil. Even Aunties that you have just met. This is Boisey and Mawe's first time meeting anyone from this side of the family, and they are very excited. Boisey, especially, is eager to meet the one other person in the world who not only has the same name, but who spells it the same, too: my uncle Boisey Christopher Collins.

This is my second visit with Annette at her house in Redford, Michigan. I first met her in 1998, more than twenty years ago, with my boyfriend at the time. *You can ask me anything about your father, and the family. Really, it's okay.* What a strange thing to hear a phrase you have longed to hear your whole life, and then to not be able to respond—at least in the moment.

"You sure all you want is some water?" Annette asks, coming out of the kitchen. She is sipping some kind of fancy mixed drink I have never heard of. "I can make you anything you want."

I shake my head, smiling a bit uncomfortably. In my teens, even before I knew anything about Patricia and her history of alcoholism, much less met her, I decided that I did not want to drink. From a distance, watching my peers, it seemed like an activity that yielded small benefits for its price. I have not been around many people who are drunk in my life, but when I have been, it has been supremely embarrassing for me in the moment, and for them later. "I'm fine," I tell Annette now.

When I was here last time, she told me something of the family's struggles with addiction. One of her sisters, Delphine, died of a heroin overdose in her twenties, and another, Barbara, died after she got sober, of complications from using heroin for so many years. My twenty-three-year-old eyes must have widened at this news, because I remember Annette shrugging matter-of-factly, and saying, "Street life got 'em."

"Okay," she says now. Her house is a modest ranch in a quiet neighborhood, a two-bedroom with a small kitchen, living room, and dining room. A miniature Christmas tree stands to my right, behind the front window that looks out on the sidewalk. A few half-open boxes crowd the living room floor. Annette has recently retired from her job at Amtrak and is planning to do some remodeling.

My thoughts are bouncing around my cranium, sparked by so much new stimulus. I think of Patricia's house, the mostly working-class jobs their family members hold, how far they went in education. And as far as I can tell, most of my relatives on the Collins side have jobs in factories or the trades, or like Annette's adult son, are successful salespeople. Whereas I have two master's degrees, my parents have master's degrees, and they built a three-thousand-square-foot house in the woods outside of Ann Arbor.

"Annette," I say, getting out my notebook and pen. "I want to ask you about my father's bipolar disorder."

She is looking at me like I have two heads. "His *what*?"

This is the thing about digging up family history: You never know when you are going to unintentionally hit a buried but still live electrical line. "Um, Christopher told me about it when we talked on the phone back in September . . ."

She scowls. "I don't know what he's talking about. I never heard anything about that."

I lean back and purse my lips. "You didn't?"

She shakes her head. "And how would he know, anyway . . . ?"

There is so much contained within that sentence. So much history I know I will never unpack.

"Hello!" a deep voice calls from the kitchen.

Boisey Christopher, or simply Christopher, as he's called here, has arrived.

"Hey!" Annette and I both say at the same time.

And just like that, our conversation about this topic is ended.

I jump up from the couch and follow Annette into the kitchen. A middle-aged Black man stands before me, maybe a little older than I am, with a wide chest and a muscular frame. Come to think of it, he kind of looks like one of those bodybuilders on TV. His legs look like long tree trunks, anchored into the ground.

"Hey, Shannon," he says, and extends his hand.

"Hi, Christopher," I say, and take it.

His grip is firm, but detached.

It's always a little odd when you finally meet someone in person who you have only spoken to over the phone or corresponded with over email. A little like a phantom made flesh. Even odder when that person is your long-lost uncle who is just four years older than you.

"Boisey," I say to my son. "Meet the only other person alive with your same name, Boisey with a 'y.'"

My son cocks his head to the right and grins at me, then at Christopher. "Yeah, because I was named after your dad, but he's dead," he says, in that upbeat tone that only a nine-year-old can use to deliver commentary about a loved one's passing.

"Hmm," I say, taking my son in a headlock, and rubbing his scalp. "That's quite a statement."

He laughs, then squirms away from me. "Yeah, but a true one, right?"

I look apologetically from Christopher to Annette. Luckily, they appear to be amused.

"Yes, that's right," I tell him. "But also, your grandfather was named Boisey, along with my father and your uncle here. So, it's quite the family name."

Christopher nods. "It's a good name," he says. "A very good name."

"Boisey! Boisey! Boisey!" his four year-old sister exclaims beside him.

Boisey rolls his eyes, in mock annoyance. "Enough, Mawe."

I laugh. "Yes, we are *so* over it." I lean over and kiss her on the forehead. Even though they exhaust and frustrate me, my children tether me to the earth so tightly that I feel held up and supported, living this particular story. Most days, there is nothing I am more thankful for.

In a few minutes, Annette's son Ron arrives, along with his wife, Angelina. We chat for a while, making pleasantries and sipping the drinks that Annette expertly keeps coming. They ask me about my work, I ask them about theirs, and then the conversation inevitably turns toward the book I'm writing.

"I'm just kind of collecting and digging up stories about my father and the family," I say. I am always trying to describe the book to people in a way that won't completely freak them out and reveal how weird I really am. Then I remember something. "Annette, you gave me all those documents about that huge family reunion that happens every few years down South?"

She nods. "I gave that to you at that first visit, right?"

I nod and sit up taller. "That was incredible. I mean, the whole thing was incredible, to have that kind of family history documented, celebrated, and handed down intergenerationally. Like, *no* Black families have that. And very few adoptees have that, either. You know how many of my adoptee friends would kill for an extensive family tree like that?"

They look at me blankly and shake their heads.

"Have you ever been?" I ask.

Everyone shakes their head again.

"I been meaning to go for years," Annette says. "Wanted to take Ron and the kids. Just never could seem to get everything together to make it happen."

I nod. "Yeah. I know what you mean."

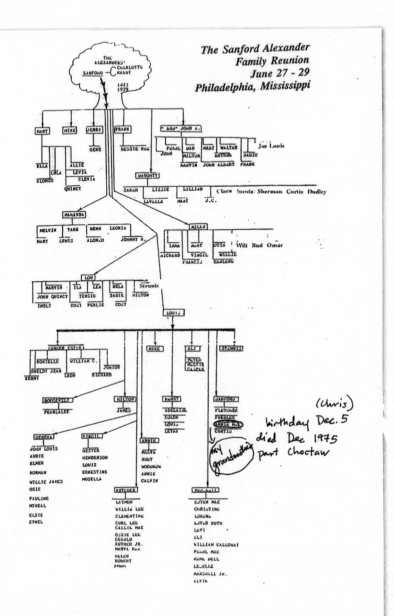

Sanford family tree from the 1997 Sanford family reunion.

Sanford Alexander Sr.

WIVES:

Charlotte and Mandy

CHILDREN:

Mike Alexander
Maranda Alexander Donald
Mary Louise (Lou) Alexander Hall
Miles Alexander
Louis Alexander
Jerry Alexander
John "Bud" Alexander
Daughty Alexander McClain
Mary Alexander Pollock

SANFORD ALEXANDER SR. was born a slave in South Carolina in 1823. The date of his exact arrival in the Sandtown Community in Neshoba County near the Bogue Chitto Community is not known. He was purchased at a slave market in New Orleans, Louisiana, by the Alexander family and brought to the area. Sanford was freed in 1865 in Neshoba County, Mississippi, at the age of forty-two. He lived sixty-four years as a free man in Neshoba and Kemper Counties. Sanford was the father of ten children from two marriages, thus expanding the Alexander name for over eight generations.

Sanford was a successful farmer who acquired several hundred acres of land. The offspring of this former slave are productive citizens who are proud of their heritage. His grandchildren, great-grandchildren, great-great-grandchildren and great-great-great-grandchildren are successful lawyers, doctors, corporate managers, computer programmers, pilots, professional football players, cattle ranchers, insurance agents, underwriters, educators and entrepreneurs. He died in 1929, at the age of 106.

Sanford was buried in the Liberty United Methodist Church Cemetery in Collinsville, Mississippi. His grandson, the late Kutcher Threefoot Alexander Sr. purchased a memorial headstone for his grave. Kutcher Threefoot Alexander found and preserved a portrait of our great-grandfather.[3]

3. Unknown member of the Sandford Alexander family, family reunion handout and family tree, 1997

Erin Powers is twenty.

WE DON'T TALK WHILE WE'RE DRIVING. Boisey Christopher has a Bronco modified for off-roading, and it's full of cardboard boxes and plastic bins. I decide not to ask him what that's all about—maybe he keeps a mobile office?—and step up into the high seat beside him. It's been a while since I've been in a truck like this. Mom always said they're too dangerous. For someone who engaged in risky behavior for all of her adult life, she certainly had a lot to say on all the ways *I* could potentially bite it. Boisey Christopher gets us on the highway in just a few minutes, and soon a swarm of cars is flying by us.

"Jesus," I say under my breath. *And I thought New York drivers were bad.* These people are all going eighty, ninety miles an hour, zipping across lanes, cutting people off right and left. I shake my head, imagining Mom's reaction.

We are clearly in an industrial part of the city, with tons of nondescript gray and brown factory buildings that you would probably miss if you didn't know what to look for. Living in Utica, I know, because we have tons of them there, too.

Then he exits, and we are on a very busy main drag, with gas stations and auto repair shops and fast food everywhere. "Ah, good ol' Eight Mile," he says with a grin. "You know you almost home once you hit it."

I nod absently. I'm thinking about what clues, if any, I should be on the lookout for once we get to my father's old lab. What the hell kind of machines do particle physicists use, anyway? I scowl, wishing I had paid more attention in physics class in high school.

"Yeah, we in the old hood now," he says, and I can see he is already revisiting some potent family memories, because he is laughing to himself. "All us kids, born and raised. Grew up, got into scrapes, moved out, got into scrapes." Then his voice gets lower, softer. "But Pops did the best he could with us."

He stops at a light, and an older Black lady crosses, pushing a grocery cart full of bags. Boisey Christopher waves at her as she walks, and she waves back.

The light changes, and we are off again. "Yeah, I never did set foot in your dad's infamous lab, but Kenny pointed it out to me one time after we went out for drinks."

I make a mental note. *Kenny, my father's younger brother, and Boisey Christopher's older one.*

He points to a warehouse about three blocks away from us. "He'd dropped Junior offa there plenty of times." He laughs. "And picked him up, after a series of all-nighters testing some top secret project." Boisey Christopher pulls up to the curb beside the warehouse and parks the car. "Yeah, I tell ya, your dad was one interesting cat."

I glare at him. I am familiar with this meaning of *interesting*.

Boisey Christopher holds up his hands. "He was brilliant! Definitely brilliant," he says. "But I'm sorry, Erin, he wasn't all there all the time." He sighs. "Which is just one of about a million reasons why this little field trip is so futile. Sorry to tell you. Again."

I step out of the car into the bright afternoon sunlight. The slam of my door is my response to him. I squint into the sky, enjoying the warmth of the sunlight on my face. Even the light here feels different than it does in Utica. More diffuse, somehow.

We begin to walk toward the warehouse, which is just as run-down as he said it would be. Its roof is partially caved in, and most of the windows are broken. Dirt and wood and metal scraps are piled all around the front and sides of the building, whose walls stretch at least a hundred feet into the air.

Boisey Christopher shakes his head, taking it all in.

"You mind?" I ask, lighting a cigarette. I only have three left, but if this moment doesn't call for one, I don't know what does.

He eyes me somewhat warily, but nods. "Didn't know you were into that."

I laugh at the absurdity.

I inhale and allow the smoke to fill my lungs. Then I exhale, enjoying the warmth of the smoke as it gathers around me.

We reach the door, or at least the remains of the door, which is charred and nearly broken in two—like some giant blade sliced through the metal.

"What the fuck? What happened here?" I say, and then instantly regret swearing. I don't know Boisey Christopher well enough to know how he will react.

But he doesn't even hear me, because he begins to kick ferociously at the door.

"Stop!" I yell, and he puts his foot down right away.

"What are the hell are you doing?"

He points at the busted-up remains in front of us. "Trying to make us an opening to get in. What does it look like I'm doing?"

I take one last drag of my cigarette, then crunch it under my foot. "That's not going to work," I tell him. "The door's too thick, and it's not all the way broken."

He frowns, peering closely at the scorch marks all over the door. "Yeah, you're probably right."

I nod my head to the right. *I'm* always *right. I just wish more people would realize that.* "Let's go around this way. See if we can find a broken window low enough to crawl through."

Boisey Christopher looks at me incredulously but follows.

There are shards of glass and metal everywhere—some of them sharp, so you have to be very careful where you step. Pieces of chairs and cabinets and even carpets litter the ground as well.

"It's like . . . something exploded inside, and just blew the hell outta the place," I say.

"What a mess," Boisey Christopher says behind me.

Then I see it. A window maybe ten feet off the ground that is three-fourths of the way broken, and large enough for me to crawl through if I stand on Boisey Christopher's shoulders. "There," I tell him, pointing to it.

He nods, and I know he knows what I'm thinking. We get close to the window, he laces his fingers together and bends down in front of me, and I step up. I climb onto his shoulders, somewhat awkwardly, but he is strong and helps me keep my balance. Once my feet are firmly on his shoulders, his hands holding me in place, I stand up slowly to face the window. I wrap my hand in my sweatshirt under my jacket, and then punch out the remaining glass. Then I peer over and onto what looks like the main floor of the warehouse.

"What do you see?" Boisey Christopher asks, below me.

There's just debris everywhere, scattered across the floor and the walls. A small desk sits against the far wall, and though its edges are charred, it appears to still be mostly intact. There are even papers strewn across it that might be readable up close. A huge metal tube sits in the middle of the open floor, badly burned and bent in places. This piques my interest, because it is connected to a strange spiral contraption on one side and what looks like a small control station on the other. If someone messes with quantum particles in a comic book or movie, the gadgets generally look like this.

I tell Boisey Christopher what I see, and ask him to give me a push up on the count of three. "One, two . . . ," he says.

"Three!" I yell, and hoist my upper body against the window frame. I press my hands downward, and pull my butt into the side of the window, praying that I haven't missed a shard of glass.

"Go, go, go!" Boisey Christopher yells below me. "You got this! You got it."

I bite my lip, trying to fold my legs up into, and then on the other side of, the window. This whole exercise reminds me of climbing with Essie at Table Rock in our teens. We would head out on Saturday mornings when my mom or her sister were driving us nuts, and just spend the day hanging off ledges and reaching for good holds. I feel a pang of longing, wishing she were here, but I let it pass. I let go, and trust my body to land me without breaking.

Boom. The ground gives a bit and a cloud of dust rises. I land on my feet, but then fall backward onto my butt.

"Erin! Erin! Are you okay?" Boisey Christopher calls from outside.

I am coughing because of the dust, trying to catch my breath. But when I take inventory of my body, I find that nothing's hurt. I just landed hard.

"Erin!" he calls again, and this time his voice is downright agitated.

I swallow, and make a real effort to get my coughing under control. "I'm fine!" I yell. "Just gimme a minute." I dust off my hands, legs, and butt. Then I stand up and survey the landscape. Inside it's even more busted up than you can see from the outside. There's water damage all over the walls. A huge poster—schematics of some kind, but nothing I can decipher—still hangs across the wall in front of me. At least a third of it has been burned off. Inspecting the floor more closely, I see that it is just dirt with a thin covering of some of white particles. *Probably some kind of toxic chemical. Nothing to worry about.* I laugh to myself.

Bam! Bam! Bam!

I jump.

I run to the front door, maybe fifty feet to my left. The doorknob has been partially melted into the door itself. *No wonder we couldn't get the damn thing open.*

"Just hold on!" I shout to Boisey Christopher from the other side. "Back up."

I can see his shadow through the huge cut in the door, retreating a bit.

I grab the doorknob, try to turn it, and lean my shoulder into the door. It doesn't want to turn and is clearly jammed. But I'm not giving up. "Fucking come on!" I yell, and in that moment, the door bursts open, and I tumble out.

Boisey Christopher laughs, and I do, too.

"This place is just a nightmare," he says.

I stand up slowly, and dust myself off again. "To us it's a nightmare. But for him, it must have been a dream realized in a lifetime of dreams lost." I walk back through the door, taking in the expansiveness of what my father made his laboratory, the light shining brightly through its many windows, the ceiling so high you would need a crane to reach it. It must have been an explosion of possibility for him, like entering another world every time he came here.

Boisey Christopher follows me, and for a moment we are both quiet, taking it all in. Plastic barrels of something line the far wall, and wooden boards are scattered across the floor. And we are kicking up dust and dirt from the floor with each step we take.

I wander over to the wall on my left, where the remains of the giant schematic hangs. There are all kinds of drawings of various pieces and parts I don't recognize at all. They are meticulously drawn in red pen, with words like "collider one," "collider two," "cyclotron," and "proton stabilizer." *Oh my God. He might have actually done it.*

Boisey Christopher stands beside me, inspecting the schematics with equal amounts fascination and shock. "Yeah, that's Junior's writing all right."

I look at him sideways. "Really?"

He nods. "Pretty unmistakable, really." He reaches out and touches the writing on the paper, almost as if this small, intimate gesture could conjure my father, in the flesh.

Butterflies gather in my stomach. I follow the words farther down on the page, to something that says, "<u>TO OPEN THE DOOR</u>." I point to it, and Boisey Christopher crowds around me, reading it, too.

1. *Start the collider.*
2. *Aim the particle beam.*
3. <u>*STAND BACK!!!*</u>
4. *Measure the ANEC.*
5. *Turn up the engine to HIGH.*
6. *Wait for door to appear.*
7. *Walk through.*

"Walk through?" Boisey Christopher says beside me. His brow is furrowed. "What the hell does that mean?"

But I understand. "Walk through," I say.

He looks at me like I am crazy, so I laugh.

"Walk through the door," I say.

"What door?"

I walk quickly across the cavernous room, to the small control console by the metal tube and spiral contraption. A box, at least thirty feet in height and width, with what looks like an engine inside it, sits to the right of the console. It is covered in spiderwebs, dirt, and those strange white particles. I realize with a start that it is just an old gasoline-powered generator. Grandma had one at the ready for snowstorms, and Uncle Jim showed me how to use it. I dust it off, and find a small button on the side, labeled "On." There is a cord beside it, and I pull it hard three times. As soon as I do, the whole building is engulfed by a deafening roar. The console beside it lights up, and begins its own, significantly quieter hum.

Boisey Christopher is holding his hands over his ears, walking toward me. "What the hell are you doing?" he yells once he is beside me.

I glare at him. "Isn't it obvious? I'm going to make the door. And then I'm going to walk through it."

PART SEVEN

"Walk through."

An Adoptee Always Precedes
a New Timeline

i.

IN THE 2018 MOVIE *AVENGERS: ENDGAME,* the character Tony Stark initially refuses to even try to solve the problem of time travel in order to save half the galaxy, for fear of losing his five-year-old biological daughter in the process. Later the same day, while looking at pictures of his own long-dead father and of Peter Parker (the young superhero who was a quasi-adopted son to Stark before Parker was lost in the cataclysm that wiped out half the galaxy), Stark seems to reconsider his choice. Moments later, he solves the problem of time travel.

ii.

A FEW DAYS LATER, in order to test Stark's time travel portal, fellow superhero Hawkeye, also known as Clint Barton, volunteers to go back in time for one minute and then return. For reasons the movie never explains, he goes back to a point on the timeline before his teenage daughter was lost in the cataclysm, and is able to remain long enough to hear her voice and to call her name before he's agonizingly snatched back to the present.

iii.

WHEN STARK AND HIS FELLOW AVENGERS actually use the time travel portal to save the people lost in the cataclysm, the first unforeseen obstacle their plan encounters comes in the form of a transracial adoptee: Loki. The child of frost giants raised by Norse gods absconds with the prized Tesseract cube after the time-traveling Avengers attempt to steal it. The Tesseract takes Loki to the Mongolian Gobi Desert, where the obtuse bureaucratic organization Time Variance Authority (TVA) finds him. The TVA imprisons Loki at their facility, and eliminates the new timeline he has created—all in order to stave off the collapse of the multiverse. Or so we are told . . .

Erin Powers is twenty.

THE OVERGROWN GENERATOR and ancient control console make such a racket that I can barely hear my own thoughts.

Boisey Christopher grabs my arm. "We have to turn it off!" he yells in my ear. "It isn't safe."

I smile and shake my head. There's no way I'm turning this thing off now. I'm too close. With a shudder, I realize that this must have been what my father felt right before he disappeared: a combustible mixture of excitement and fear.

Boisey Christopher studies my profile.

I can see he is trying to decide how to respond, which means I might not have much time. I scan the control console and find a big "On" button. But it is covered in an X of red tape. I move my hand to press it.

"No, don't!" Boisey Christopher yells.

But I am too fast. I hit the button with all my might.

At first, nothing happens. What I mean is, nothing *new* happens. The generator and control console are still screaming in our ears.

"Thank God," says Boisey Christopher. "You probably coulda—"

And then it begins: A low hum initially. Then a rattle and a pop, a machine getting into gear, and then a whirring sound comes from the huge metal tube. It gets louder and louder with each second, until it eclipses even the sound of the generator.

"What the fuck did you *do*?" Boisey Christopher yells at me. Only, I have to read his lips, because I can't hear him at all.

He grabs my arm again, and tries to pull me away from the console, toward the door. "Time to go!"

I shake my head and try to push him off. "No!" I plant my feet into the dirt and grasp the sides of the console.

A crashing noise erupts behind us. I turn and see that a window has exploded, its shards ricocheting across the room. Then there is another crash, and another, and another. The collider, or whatever it is, is exploding all the glass in the vicinity, window by window. I shriek as a shard slices my cheek. Beside me, I hear Boisey Christopher gasp. Then, suddenly, a huge beam of light is emitted from the tube, and all the glass stops breaking. The light is orange and yellow and white and is only about a foot in diameter. It has an eerie translucent glow and occasionally pops with sparks.

Boisey Christopher and I slowly rise from our hunched positions at the console, mesmerized by the beam.

"Jesus," he says, brushing off shards of glass. "What is that?"

I walk toward the beam slowly, my right hand out.

"Erin . . . what are you going to do?" He starts to walk behind me, then thinks better of it, and stops.

I don't answer him, because the closer I get to the beam, the more it starts to feel so familiar. Until I am right beside it, and I can see her, I mean me—the Other Me—a teenager sitting at a table with Mom over tea, and to the side of that, a kid running with two boys into the woods. I can hear her, too. She's laughing, and then saying, *No, I know it was her.*

"Erin, stop!" Boisey Christopher yells.

I turn to face him for a moment. He has a gash across his forehead, and another on his left arm. I feel bad for dragging him into all of this.

Erin! I'm here.

I whip around, my eyes huge, my heart pounding. That voice came from the beam, and that voice was him. That voice was my father.

Shannon! I'm here.

Him again. *I think that's her name.*

I rush to the beam, so that I'm almost touching it. And I can see my father there inside it, sitting on a park bench somewhere, looking right at me. Bright eyes, radiant brown skin, and warm smile, waiting.

But I sense that there is something missing. Something I've forgotten. *2. Aim the particle beam.* Inside the beam, my father nods, and points to the cone beside the metal tube. I run over to it and push it closer, so that the beam can go through. *Don't touch the beam!* my father yells. I very carefully maneuver the cone after that, keeping it between the beam and me. *Yes,* he says. *Like that.*

Once the beam is focused, I walk back to the console, and find the knob labeled "Low," "Medium," and "High." Boisey Christopher is beside me, and I don't know if he's seen or heard my father, too, but he pats me on the shoulder, and steps back. It's like he gets it now. I turn the knob all the way to high, and the beam expands twofold, and begins to churn into a spiral on the wall it hits. It fizzes and sparks, and a shimmering kind of passage opens. It is mirrorlike, waving back and forth.

"The wormhole," I whisper. "The door."

Completely mesmerized, I walk toward it. My father stands up from his seat on the bench and beckons me. *I've been waiting for you,* he says. His smile is contagious and reminds me of my son's: all the teeth perfectly lined up and shiny. The wormhole shudders a bit, the closer I get. Its sides appear to be solid, but when I touch it, there is nothing there. My hand feels like it's just touching air. *He's got one trick to last a lifetime, and that's all a pony needs,* someone sings from inside. It's her! It's me, with a frizzy fourth-grade afro, my hand-me-down pink-and-gray shorts, faded Muppets T-shirt, and broken-down loafers. We are standing on the side of a busy highway somewhere inside the wormhole, dancing and singing "One-Trick Pony." Farther away, my father—another version of my father?—stands, looking at fourth-grade us incredulously. And I have the strongest feeling that this has all happened before. My father, the one maybe a foot in front of me, on the edge of the wormhole, offers his hand to me. I think of all the times in my life I have wanted to take hold of him, even for just a moment. To see if my flesh was in fact reflected in his. And now, here we are! It is happening. *It's okay,* he says. *I promise.* I look back at Boisey Christopher, still standing at the console.

He nods. He is cut and bleeding and dirty and generally as busted up as I am, but he is here. "Go," he says simply.

I turn back to my father. His hand is luminous and shimmery, his nails bitten. I take a deep breath and grab his hand. Then I wait for all the atoms in my body to implode. Or for his hand to absorb mine. Or for time to start flowing backward. *It doesn't work that way, silly,* says fourth-grade us again, laughing. Since none of that happens, I step into the wormhole entirely, still holding on to him. It's like I'm in a tube on a water slide, but it's a lot fancier. The walls continue to sizzle and spark, and are a bright silver color inside. I look down to see what I'm standing on, but there is no ground. It's like we're just float- ing in the wormhole. I gasp, lose my balance, and fall over. My father laughs. *Happens to everyone,* he says. *Gotta get your wormhole legs.* I carefully bring my hands down to my sides, and push on whatever is there, since it isn't ground. Whatever it is, particles of some sort, pushes back on me, and in an instant I am standing again. I look up as a kaleidoscope of lights shoots up above us. *A meteor shower in a nearby galaxy,* my father says. His hand is firm and feels as real as any other hand I have held. I close my eyes. *This can't be happening. This can't be happening.* He reaches up and takes my chin. *Why not?* he asks, looking into my eyes. *Multiple timelines are always unfolding in multiple universes, with infinite versions of you. I have been here for almost fifteen of what you in your universe call years, watching you grow, watching you question, watching you learn and play.* I pull back from him, shock clouding my face. *But why?* I ask. *I don't understand.* If that's true, this wormhole must arrest the aging process, because he doesn't look a day over thirty-five. He nods and gestures for me to follow him over to his bench. I step on nothing, to nowhere, and we sit down on the bench. Once we are seated, I can see two small passages right in front of us—small sub-tunnels of the wormholes. I squint at the right one and can just barely make out two young white kids, running and throwing things in a house. *What the hell . . . ?* I say, starting to get up. But my father rests his arm across my lap, stopping me. *Don't,* he says. *They're just time loops.* He shrugs. *Nothing to worry about.* I frown at him. He has to know I have no idea what he's talking about. *Is* she *on the other side of one of them?* I ask, and I can't help the accusatory tone. My father, full of surprises, smiles. *No, not at all.* He waves his hand. *Don't worry about her. You'll meet her soon enough.* My stomach falls. *I will?* I grab his hand, hard. *Where? When? And who is she, anyway?* He looks at me in confusion. *You know who she is, Erin.* I eye him sideways, suddenly angry. *I do not. I've been trying to find out who she is for years.* My father squeezes my hand, and then kisses my forehead. His lips are dry and sweet. My eyes are wet. *She's you, sweetie.* My breath catches in my throat. He looks at me sadly, and nods. *And also not you. I mean . . . it all depends on if you believe in a discrete definition of "you" anyway. Or discrete timelines and universes . . . After all, I've been popping in and out of the ancillary regions of this wormhole for eons, occasionally bumping into myself. Which is as weird as it sounds . . .* His eyebrows become quite animated when he talks about something that fascinates him. And he starts moving his hands everywhere.

A loud snapping noise to my right jolts me. I look in the direction that it came from, and I see that a spiral has appeared, exactly like the one on my bathroom mirror ten years ago, at the point where the wormhole and warehouse meet. The spiral begins to churn and pop, going faster with each rotation. *What in the . . . ?* I whisper. *Shit,* says my father. *We have even less time than I thought.* I feel my eyes become large saucers. *What the hell does that mean?* I ask. He shakes his head and grabs my hands. *Listen, Erin. I need you and Shannon to know that this whole thing: the collider, me residing here after my disappearance on your timeline, and after my death on hers. . . . All of it I did because of you.* I can feel my hand actually sweating in his, which confuses me. And my head is pounding. *I don't understand, Dad,* I say. He smiles at the word, and I notice for the first time that crinkles appear at the corners of his eyes when he does. But then his face goes hard again, and he clasps my fingers so hard I think he might break them. *Yes, I got obsessed with the possibility of opening a door to a wormhole here, in college, on this timeline. But I never really believed it was possible until you—I mean, Shannon—went through that time loop and found me. The one she's about to go through now, singing that Paul Simon song . . . That was all on her timeline, and I didn't even know it was just months before my death.* I shake my head, my thoughts jumbled. *You're not making sense, Dad. I don't know what this is about . . .*

Boom! The spiral on the end of the wormhole emits a deafening rumble, and the walls begin to shake. *The structural integrity can't withstand both you and me inside this at the same time,* he says. He pulls me up from the bench and pulls me toward the spiral. *No! Dad, please! I just got here.* We are almost to its center. *You have to go now; otherwise, you might never exist,* he says, but his words are getting fuzzy in my ears. We are standing on the precipice, and I can see Boisey Christopher standing on the other side, in the warehouse, a tiny insignificant dot in the fabric of space-time. Just like me. Just like him. Just like Mom, Shannon, and whoever else she has on her side. He holds my face in his hands, one last time. *Listen to me, baby girl. It doesn't matter who you are in this universe or any other. You're all mine, baby.*

All. Mine. And I've loved you your whole life, even before I knew you existed. I'm crying now, as he pushes me away from him. *It was always you, Erin! Shannon! You are the reason the timelines got all botched and we could meet here, only for a moment. Thank God. After you came through the wormhole to meet me on that highway all those years ago, you showed me what was possible. So, I built it. I built the collider, which opened the door to the wormhole. If you hadn't come and met me there, I never would have followed through.*

When I come to, I'm lying in the dirt of the warehouse, a halo of white particles floating around me. After all the noise of the generator and collider, it is eerily quiet now. I sit straight up, taking a jagged breath, and see the busted console, and the metal tube of the collider, split in two. The spiral coil is fractured as well, and all that remains of the beam and the wormhole inside it is a burned circle on the far wall.

"Erin!" someone yells.

In a minute, Boisey Christopher is beside me. "What the hell happened? One minute you were here, the next all I could see was this blinding bright light . . ." He scoops me up, and carries me out of the warehouse, back to the car. I let him, and even rest my head on his chest. I'm not surprised to feel the wetness of tears on my cheeks.

My father is gone again, and yet he is not. Just like her. Just like Mom.

Shannon Gibney is ten.

DINNER OVER, she stands up and begins clearing the plates. It is her turn this week, Ben's turn to set the table, and Jon's turn to empty the dishwasher. Mom and Dad have created a reliable list of chores which the kids follow to the punctuation mark. And argue over relentlessly.

She carries the plates, dirty with the remains of bean burritos, to the kitchen counter, two at a time. It is six o'clock, and the autumn air has a brisk quality of anticipation that is so enticing. Out in the backyard, Sandy, our sheltie, barks at something. The bark itself is short and clipped—like she has found something she shouldn't get into. I press my face against the cool glass of the sliding door that faces the backyard, intentionally smushing my nose and lips. Eddie Taylor called them "banana lips" at recess last week right before I tagged him, and it felt like he smacked me. I don't know why.

Jon and Ben have retreated to their room, ostensibly to play Legos. And Mom and Dad are in the den below, talking in hushed tones about something of grown-up importance. Sandy barks again, and now I see her approaching the end of the backyard and the beginning of the woods. The girl peers at the dog carefully and is sure she sees a small flicker of light in the woods, cradled by branches and ground. She wonders if the spiral, the portal could finally be back. The tips of her fingers tingle at the thought.

The dog walks stealthily to the edge of the tree line, sniffs the air, and then takes off toward the light. "Sandy!" the girl calls, but she knows it is pointless, the sound muffled by the glass door. So, she opens it, and steps into the cool autumn night. The mosquitoes haven't been killed by the frost yet, but even they can't spoil the simple beauty of the evening. It's a harvest moon, casting a luminous yellow glow over the grass, picnic table, and treehouse. But it still doesn't dull the bright light coming from the woods, growing in power and diameter every moment. "Sandy!" she calls again, and hears a rustling somewhere in the woods. Her feet start walking, slowly at first but then incrementally faster and more urgently, toward the woods, the dog, and the light. It is a cold evening, colder than she anticipated, and she rubs her forearms with her hands. In a minute, she is at the forest's edge. Sandy barks more forcefully this time, and Shannon sees her near the light. She's definitely barking at it, but at this vantage point, she can't see what the light actually is. My breath caught in my windpipe, I lift up my right foot and then my left. I am in the woods, Sandy a few feet in front of me, agitated and pacing in front of a small circle with a spiral center, moving on the forest floor. It is bright, sending out mostly white light, but occasionally she can see specks of violet and blue and even green.

"Oh my God," she whispers. "It's back."

I can't help myself and move closer to it, as Sandy backs away. Just like last spring, the spiral seems to be growing with each rotation, throwing off more light and even emitting a sound as it turns. It's a high-pitched noise that is barely perceptible.

It feels like the spiral is pulling me to it, and like I'm pulling it to me. She peers at it, and sees two shimmering tunnels, one leading to a grown-up woman who looks suspiciously like me, in some kind of warehouse looking back through the long tunnel at her, and the other leading to a frustrated grown-up Black man with a busted car on the side of the highway somewhere. Her eyes open wide. "It's him," she says. "It's my father." She doesn't know how she knows this. She just does.

The girl looks back longingly at the small house with the sliding glass door, and the three bedrooms sandwiched together on the second floor. She can see her brothers building something on their bed, and farther down in the den, the light makes shadows of her parents leaning forward in their seats. *This is my home,* the girl thinks. *Who I belong to.* And she believes it. And yet, when she turns back to the spiral and the tunnel leading to him, she cannot deny that he belongs to her, too. With his sad eyes and agitated hands. *I have to go. I hope to return, but I have to go.*

I touch the spiral and a giant spark goes off. It feels like an electrical current rips up my body, and the spiral starts sputtering and spitting. It turns on its side, and the escalating high-pitched noise is all-encompassing for a minute, making me feel like my head might explode. Then there is a small popping noise, and I know what will happen if I don't do something. So I take a step. I walk through.

Afterward

Life on Planet Adoptee

*Group text thread including Sun Yung Shin, Kimberly McKee
(both writers and Korean adoptees), Sarah Park Dahlen (Korean
American critical adoption and children's literature scholar), and
Shannon Gibney, February 5, 2022.*

SUN YUNG SHIN: *"This uncertainty over when a birth date
may initially seem like a clerical error, however, I argue it
reflects the ways in which biographical details are seen as
fungible and mutable as part of the orphan manufacturing
process."* [Quoting from Kimberly McKee's book
Disrupting Kinship]

KIMBERLY MCKEE: *I just think we need to think about those
social workers at Korean agencies as the original adoption
creative fiction writers.*

SYS: *Yes.*

KM: *Like who created those stock templates.*

It was a skill.

SYS: *I think my surname is Shin because allegedly there was a
policeman who found me named Shin. But also the police
box was romanized as Shinkyo in my paperwork.*

*. . . BUT who knows if I was even dropped off at that
police station, right—*

SARAH PARK DAHLEN: *Stock templates—orphan templates that Deann talks about in Cha Jung Hee* [Deann Borshay Liem's 2010 film, *In the Matter of Cha Jung Hee*].

KM: *I think some of this depends on when you were adopted/ relinquished.*

Some things are more plausible.

SPD: *I mean even people who reunite aren't sure they have the whole story . . . look at Lisa Sjoblom* [Lisa Wool-Rim Sjöblom, author of *Palimpsest: Documents from a Korean Adoption*].

SYS: *Yes.*

KM: *My Omma* ["mom" in Korean] *experienced a lot of PTSD once we reunited.*

SYS: *Layers of lies and sadness.*

Heartbreaking.

KM: *My paternal halmoni* ["grandmother" in Korean] *also wanted my omma to have an abortion. My omma told me that and then said we're also going to Costco.*

SHANNON GIBNEY: *Yep, that's how it goes.*

In The Girl I Am, Was, and Never Will Be, *I include parts of letters my birth mom wrote me and my mom at various points, talking about how she actually went to the abortion clinic, but then couldn't go through with it. Because I "spoke" to her.*

For our entire childhoods and most of our adolescence, we thought we were the only ones. With stories too filled with holes to make any sense at all. With an abiding disbelief in the American religion of the family, of permanency, of universal middle-class happy-endings. With this particular racial and cultural shame, and an obtuse sense of humor borne of living in the heart of the heart of Empire, though not belonging to it.

But as it turned out, we were not the only ones.

"I had been an empty space, and now I was finding a language, a story to shape myself by. I had been alone and now there were others," Linda Hogan writes in her luminous novel *Solar Storms*.

Even if you only have part of your story, the shreds can still be recognized by others who are products of similar narrative fragments. Those others who also reside on Planet Adoptee—a world which we didn't even have a name for until we found each other.

We make our way through and within our stories by creating a language of recognition. It is sharp, and fragmented, anguished, and sardonic. But it is something for an adoptee to be *recognized*. To have meaning reproduced in a casual turn of phrase . . . rather than repeatedly misused or misunderstood.

We go about our business on Planet Adoptee: writing, reading, working, raising children, paying our bills. We no longer look for resolved narratives, our language of fact and possibility weaving endlessly back and forth.

Acknowledgments

This book comes from the collective labor, lived experience, storytelling, and tenacity of many individuals and communities. I am immensely thankful to all of them for whatever role they played in this journey of creation.

Specifically, thanks to my children, Boisey and Mawe, for always believing in me, and trusting me with parts of your stories. Not to mention giving me space and love to write.

Thanks to both my parents, Jim and Susan Gibney, for always believing in me and supporting me. Thanks to my brothers, Jon and Ben Gibney, for staying the course together. And extra thanks to Susan, for saving all the letters from my birth mother, Patricia Powers, over many years—and then handing them over to me, no questions asked, when I said I needed them for the book.

Thanks to the Collins family, for sharing the pieces of my birth father you have left.

Thanks to the Powers family, for welcoming me, if not my identity.

Thanks to my homegirls: Bobbi Chase Wilding, Dagny Hanner, Karen Hausdoerffer, Shalini Gupta, Sun Yung Shin, Kimberly McKee, Sarah Park Dahlen, Valérie Déus, Greta Palm, Lisa Marie Brimmer, and JaeRan Kim for your never-ending enthusiasm and sound counsel through the ups and downs of this writing life.

Thanks to the Anderson Center for providing a beautiful and nurturing space to imagine and outline the first steps of this project.

Thanks to genetic counselor and fellow adoptee Heewon Lee, for making the beautiful genetic family map for me, and then allowing me to use it in the book.

Thanks to my amazing agent, Tina Dubois, who kicks ass with a smile when necessary, and knows all the things about the publishing industry that I never want to know, so I don't have to deal with them and can just write.

Thanks to the entire team at Dutton Books for Young Readers—Julie Strauss-Gabel, Melissa Faulner, Anna Booth, Natalie Vielkind, Anne Heausler and Rob Farren—for believing in this manuscript, and doing whatever it takes to make it shine.

Thanks to my singular editor, Andrew Karre, for your brilliance and commitment to this story. As usual, you pushed me to make it better.

Thanks to Planet Adoptee and all the adoptees out there, for showing me I am okay . . . and not alone.

Resources for Further Exploration

BOOKS

Carroll, Rebecca. *Surviving the White Gaze: a Memoir.* New York: Simon & Schuster, 2022.

Chau, Adam, and Kevin Ost-Vollmers, eds. *Parenting as Adoptees.* United States: CQT Media and Publishing, and LGA Inc., 2012.

Chung, Nicole. *All You Can Ever Know.* New York: Catapult, 2018.

Gibney, Shannon. *See No Color.* Minneapolis: Carolrhoda Lab, 2015.

Gibney, Shannon and Nicole Chung, eds. *When We Become Ours: An Adoptee Anthology.* New York: HarperCollins, 2023.

Harness, Susan Devan. *Bitterroot: A Salish Memoir of Transracial Adoption.* Lincoln: University of Nebraska Press, 2020.

Harris, Susan O'Connor, Diane Renee Christian, and Mei-Mei Akwai, eds. *Black Anthology: Adult Adoptees Claim Their Space.* Seattle, WA: CreateSpace, 2016.

Kay, Jackie. *The Adoption Papers.* Hexham, UK: Bloodaxe Books, 1991

Lockington, Mariama. *For Black Girls Like Me.* New York: Farrar, Straus and Giroux, 2019.

McKee, Kimberly. *Disrupting Kinship: Transnational Politics of Korean Adoption in the United States.* Urbana: University of Illinois Press, 2019.

McKinley, Catherine. *The Book of Sarahs: A Family in Parts.* New York: Counterpoint, 2002.

Nelson, Kim Park. *Invisible Asians: Korean American Adoptees, Asian American Experiences, and Racial Exceptionalism.* New Bunswick: Rutgers University Press, 2016.

Raleigh, Elizabeth. *Selling Transracial Adoption: Families, Markets, and the Color Line.* Philadelphia: Temple University Press, 2017.

Roorda, Rhonda M. *In Their Voices: Black Americans on Transracial Adoption*. New York: Columbia University Press, 2015.

Salesses, Matthew. *Disappear Doppelgänger Disappear*. New York: Little A Books, 2020.

Shin, Sun Yung. *Unbearable Splendor*. Minneapolis: Coffee House Press, 2016.

Trenka, Jane Jeong, Julia Chinyere Oparah, and Sun Yung Shin, eds. *Outsiders Within: Writing on Transracial Adoption*. Minneapolis: University of Minnesota Press, 2021.

Trenka, Jane Jeong. *The Language of Blood*. Minneapolis: Graywolf Press, 2005.

Trenka, Jane Jeong. *Fugitive Visions: An Adoptee's Return to Korea*, Minneapolis: Graywolf Press, 2009.

Tucker, Angela. *"You Should Be Grateful": Stories of Race, Identity, and Transracial Adoption*. Boston: Beacon Press, 2023.

Vincent, A.A. *Person, Perceived Girl*. New York: Barrow Street Press, 2022.

Wills, Jenny Heijun. *Older Sister. Not Necessarily Related*. New York: McClelland & Stewart, 2019.

Wool-Rim Sjöblom, Lisa. *Palimpsest: Documents from a Korean Adoption*. Montreal: Drawn and Quarterly, 2019.

FILMS

A Story of One's Own. Directed by Amandine Gay, 2021.

Blood Memory: A Story of Removal and Return. Directed by Drew Nicholas, 2019.*

Closure. Directed by Bryan Tucker, 2013.

First Person Plural. Directed by Deann Borshay, 2000.

Geographies of Kinship. Directed by Deann Borshay, 2019.

Girl, Adopted. Directed by Melanie Judd and Susan Motamed, 2013.*

In the Matter of Cha Jung Hee. Directed by Deann Borshay, 2010.

Off and Running. Directed by Nicole Opper, 2009.*

Struggle for Identity. Directed by Deborah C. Hoard, 2007.

PODCASTS

Adapted. Hosted by Kaomi Goetz. (2016 to present, explores the experiences of Korean adoptees.)

Adopted Feels. Hosted by Hana and Ryan. (2021 to present, Australian Korean adoptees discuss anything adoption-related.)

Adoptees On. Hosted by Haley Radke. (2016 to present, adult adoptees share life stories and what they've learned.)

The Janchi Show. Hosted by Nathan Nowack, Patrick Armstrong, and K. J. Roelke. (2020 to present, by, for, and about Korean adoptees)

Labor of Love. Hosted by Nari Baker and Robyn Park. (2021 to present, adoptee parents share thoughts and insights).

WEBSITES AND BLOGS

The Adopted Ones blog: theadoptedones.wordpress.com/

Adoption Mosaic: adoptionmosaic.com

The Alliance for the Study of Adoption and Culture: adoptionandculture.org

Diary of a Not-So-Angry Asian Adoptee: diaryofanotsoangryasianadoptee.com/

Harlow's Monkey: harlows-monkey.com

I Am Adoptee (a community built around mental health and wellness): iamadoptee.org

Intercountry Adoptee Voices (ICAV): intercountryadopteevoices.com

---

*Although these three documentaries are produced by non-adoptees, I am including them here because they center Native and teenage Black female transracial adoptee experiences and voice—something that is all too uncommon.

Photo credits

All photos and documents shown in this book are courtesy of the author with the exceptions of the following images:

Page 48: The photo of Boisey Collins Jr. is courtesy of Annette Bracey.

Page 177: The genetic family tree was created for the author by Heewon Lee.

Page 180: The photo of the Collins family is courtesy of Annette Bracey.

Page 205: Documents associated with the 1997 Sanford Alexander Family Reunion are courtesy of Annette Bracey.